"You are naked in my

"I'm wearing a smile." Erick lay flat on his back with his hands behind his head...waiting.

"That doesn't count," Clover said.

Without saying another word, he kissed her. It was a deep, long, sensual kiss, much deeper and harder than he'd kissed her before. With the lights off, everything seemed to mean more, to matter more. It didn't feel like they were playing anymore.

And Erick was naked, completely, not even wearing that smile.

Tentatively she slid her hand down his chest to his stomach and stopped there while he kissed her neck under her ear.

"Take your time," he whispered. "I have all night."

Dear Reader,

When my husband and I moved out to Oregon, one of our first trips was up Mount Hood to check out the famous Timberline Lodge (as seen in *The Shining*), to Mount Hood National Forest and Lost Lake, which is the most photographed spot in the entire state. Upon arriving at Lost Lake on a fine October afternoon, we realized why. The view of the top of Mount Hood is glorious, and on a clear day you can see the snow-capped volcanic peak reflected in the deep dark blue waters of the lake. I'd never seen anything like it before. It was utterly romantic. And when a romance writer sees a place that beautiful and that romantic, she has to write a book about it. In fact, I wrote three books about it, and this is number two in the Men at Work trilogy of books set in and around Lost Lake and Mount Hood.

I hope you enjoy *Her Naughty Holiday*, featuring Clover Greene, who owns and operates a highly successful garden nursery, and Erick Fields, the father of Clover's teenaged assistant, Ruthie, who is determined to play matchmaker. Clover needs a boyfriend to get her nagging family off her back about her personal life this Thanksgiving. Meanwhile Ruthie wants a cool stepmother and has decided Clover's the woman for her. But is Clover the right woman for Erick? We'll see...

Happy reading!

Tiffany Reisz

Unofficial Ambassador to Mount Hood, Oregon

Her Naughty Holiday

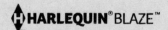

Recycling programs
for this product may
not exist in your area.

ISBN-13: 978-0-373-79920-6

Her Naughty Holiday

Copyright © 2016 by Tiffany Reisz

Printed in U.S.A.

www.Harlequin.com

Tiffany Reisz is a multi-award-winning and bestselling author. She lives on Mount Hood in Oregon in her secret volcanic lair with her husband, author Andrew Shaffer, two cats and twenty sock monkeys named Gerald. Find her online at tiffanyreisz.com.

Books by Tiffany Reisz

Harlequin Blaze

Men at Work

Her Halloween Treat

MIRA Books

The Original Sinners Series

The White Years

*

The Queen
The Virgin
The King
The Saint

The Red Years

*

The Mistress
The Prince
The Angel
The Siren

To get the inside scoop on Harlequin Blaze and its talented writers, visit Facebook.com/BlazeAuthors.

All backlist available in ebook format.

Visit the Author Profile page at Harlequin.com for more titles.

Dedicated to...

My family, who loves me for me.

1

IT WAS THE best of emails. It was the worst of emails. And Clover received them both within two minutes of each other.

Clover's emotional pendulum swung from left to right so fast upon checking her computer she had to put her head down onto her desk and breathe through the light-headedness. It was in this unusually undignified position— arms on desk, head between arms, hoodie over her head—that Clover's assistant found her.

"Um, Clo? You okay down there?"

"Oh, I'm fine. Thanks for asking."

"Are you sure you're fine?"

"Sure I'm sure."

"Are you sure you're sure you're sure?"

"Nope."

"I didn't think so."

Clover sat up and looked across her desk where her seventeen-year-old assistant, Ruthie, stood looking at her, waiting for an explanation.

"Is your hair more purple than usual today?" Clover asked. "Or is it the light?"

"More purple. I recolored it last night."

"Looks good."

"Thanks."

Clover put her head back down on her desk.

"Clover?"

"What?"

"Clove?"

"What?"

"Clo?"

"What is it, Ruthie?" Clover sat up again.

"You were moaning. Did you know that?"

"I was?"

"You were. And not the good kind of moaning."

Clover narrowed her eyes at Ruthie.

"What would you know about the good kind of moaning?" Clover asked.

"Nothing. I know nothing about good moaning. That's what we tell Pops, anyway. Right?"

"Right. Pops. Your father. Oh, God. My father…"

Once more her head hit her desk and this time it wasn't coming back up until the world had ended, thus solving all of Clover's problems.

"Clo, what's wrong? Tell me or I'm not leaving."

"You have to leave. You have a plane to catch."

"The plane is taking me to LA. Trust me, I'm in no hurry to get there."

Clover slowly rolled up and sat back in her office chair. The place was a mess, but a comfortable mess. She had ferns overflowing onto her worktable, orchids on her desk, potting soil in the wheelbarrow by the storm door and her lemon tree was getting so big it hung over her desk, making the whole office look like something out of a Dr. Seuss book. She liked it here. She loved it here. Maybe she'd stay here. Forever.

"My parents' house finally sold and my sister's

house has ants and has to be fumigated. And my brother's house is still undergoing renovations that they were undergoing last Thanksgiving."

"Good for your parents. Bad for your brother and sister."

"Also, PNW Garden Supply upped their offer to five million."

Ruthie's blue eyes went as big as the lemons hanging off Clover's tree.

"Five million dollars? For this place?"

"And the Portland location."

"This is all… Wow. But I don't get the connection between a house selling, ants, a buyout offer and…this." Ruthie flopped over onto Clover's desk before standing up again.

"The buyout offer is great, fantastic, fabulous," Clover said. "And I have until Monday to decide to take it or not."

"Tomorrow is Monday."

"Next Monday, the Monday after Thanksgiving. And with Mom and Dad out of their house and Kelly's house being fumigated, and Hunter's house being renovated… We know what that means."

"We do?"

"It means lucky me gets to host Thanksgiving. By the way, they didn't ask me if I would host Thanksgiving. No, they told me to expect them on Thanksgiving. So the week I should be deciding if I'm going to sell the company I've spent the last five years of my life building is the week I'll be hosting my family, and…oh, my God, kill me, Ruthie. Please."

Head met desk once more and they decided to spend the rest of their lives together.

"Do you need a lavender-infused wipe?" Ruthie asked.

"Yes, please."

Ruthie put the lavender-scented moist towelette into her hand, and Clover pressed it against her face and inhaled deeply and repeatedly.

"Is it working? Calmer yet?" Ruthie asked.

"Do you have anything stronger? Like chloroform?"

"I could light some incense, maybe?" Ruthie suggested. "Or we can go out and find a yew tree."

"Yew trees are not native to this continent. Also, they're highly toxic, so exactly what are we supposed to do with a yew tree?" Clover asked, narrowing her eyes behind the lavender towel. "You aren't poisoning anyone, are you?"

"Trees are ancient sacred beings, and yew trees are symbols of renewal. We should stand in front of one and ask Mother Nature for Her wisdom."

"I have this lemon tree right here." Clover pointed at the tree hanging over her head. "Is that not good enough for the Mother?"

"Fruit trees are fertility symbols. If we pray under that one you might get pregnant. Or worse, I might get pregnant."

"Okay, we'll skip the lemon tree, then. Although if I got pregnant that would shut my family up."

"Your family wants you to get pregnant?"

"They want me to be happy. It's awful."

"Yeah, sounds absolutely horrible," Ruthie said in her glorious teenage deadpan. "Screw them."

"No, it's not that. Well, it is. My brother will come to Thanksgiving and he will bring his wife, Lisa, and their three kids. My sister will bring her handsome husband and their four kids. Mom and Dad will come to

Thanksgiving and cry with joy because all their children and grandchildren are under the same roof. And I will be there. Alone. In the house. Thirty years old. No husband. No boyfriend. No kids. I haven't even been on a date in years. And they will let me know over and over again, and in no uncertain terms, that I'm not getting any younger, and if I'm ever going to be happy that magical way they are happy with their beautiful spouses and their perfect children, I have to get a move on it. And I will sit there and I will listen to all of this. And..."

"And?"

"And I will smile and nod while I mentally stab them all with the carving knife."

"Why only mentally?"

Clover looked up from the nest she'd made with her hoodie on the desk.

"You're a creepy kid, Ruthie. Just a little creepy." She held up her fingers an inch apart.

"Thank you." Ruthie curtsied.

"I knew you'd like that. So...that's what's wrong. Nothing and everything."

"Can't you just tell your family to shut up and mind their own business? It's your body, your womb."

"Why don't you just tell your dad to shut up and mind his own business when he asks you about your homework or your grades or your boyfriend?"

"I do."

"Does it work?"

"All right, you got me there. Maybe next time your mom tells you to have kids you can say you've dedicated your womb to Mother Earth."

"What does that entail exactly?"

"I don't know, but I said it at school once and it got me out of PE that day so you should try it."

"That would not go over very well with my Presbyterian mother."

"You need a new family," Ruthie said. "You can join my coven."

Clover sat up for the last time, abandoning her desk nest for good. She was a grown-up, after all. She needed to be setting a better example for Ruthie. Adults face their problems. They do not hide from them inside hooded sweatshirts.

"I love my family. I just also, sort of, hate them. Listen to this email from my sister."

Clover pulled it up and read in her best fake sweet voice.

Clo! OMG, thank you for letting us do Thanksgiving at your place. It must be so great not having kids so you have all that free time. It's a good thing I love these kids because, I swear, they are the biggest handful on earth. It must be nice only having to deal with plants. If they die nobody cares, right? I have to keep these critters alive and that is a full-time job. Speaking of the kids, I posted about fifty new pics in the family photo album. Can't wait to hear what you think of Gus's class picture. He's really the cutest kid in the class but I'm probably biased. Love you! See you Thursday!

Ruthie stared at her, wide-eyed with horror.

"I hate your family. Even Gus," Ruthie said. "Goddess forgive me."

"Fifty new pictures of the kids? She just put in two dozen last weekend! And I have to comment on every last one of them or she'll bug me until I do."

"Children are parasites," Ruthie said.

"So I'm guessing you're not planning on having kids when you're older?"

"What do you have against parasites?" Ruthie rolled her eyes.

Clover wisely chose to ask no follow-up questions.

"Nobody cares if my plants die?" Clover said with a sigh. "Does she not understand that I sell plants and I can't sell dead plants?"

"Has she met any of your customers? She should come answer the phone for a week here, and then she can say nobody cares if your plants die," Ruthie said. "Does she not know if the plants die, your business dies?"

"Kelly means well."

"You have to let me burn her house down. Please?"

"No burning anything. You're still on probation."

"Fine. But if she ever comes in here I'm going to put a Venus flytrap down her pants."

"That doesn't sound very Zen."

"Zen is a teaching of Buddhism. Although I respect Buddhism, I'm technically a neo-pagan. And neo-pagans would totally put a Venus flytrap down your sister's pants. At least this neo-pagan would."

"You're very...sweet? Okay, no, but it's nice of you to defend me. My family wants the best for me, but it's always their version of 'the best,' not my version. I know exactly what Mom will say when I tell her about the buyout offer. She'll say, 'Oh, Clo, honey, that's wonderful. Now you can quit work and finally focus on your personal life.' I'd bet money on those exact words."

"Weird. I'd say, 'Oh, Clo, that's wonderful. Five million dollars buys, like, five years of male escort services.'"

"Only five years?"

"Those guys make bank, Clo. You should hire one. He could help you with your little problem…" Ruthie sang, fluttering her eyelashes, the very picture of feigned innocence.

"I don't even feel comfortable getting manicures. Do you really think I could handle hiring a male escort? And what on earth are you doing looking up male escorts, anyway?"

"I admire them. They are the only men on the planet doing what the Goddess intends men to do, i.e., devoting themselves entirely to female pleasure."

"If I didn't let you hire a stripper for my birthday, do you really think I'm going to hire a male escort? For anything? Including my little problem or my big problem?"

"Okay, maybe not. But you could ask Pops."

"What?"

"Ask Pops. You know, my father? Picks me up every day? The tall guy with the dirt under his nails who's cute, I guess, for a dad."

"Yes, I know who your father is. We've met a few hundred times."

"Well, ask him, then. He has all his teeth and all his hair and he knows how to cook a turkey. What more could any woman want in a fake boyfriend?"

"He's your dad."

"I know. I've also met him," Ruthie said.

"I can't ask your dad to help me with my little problem."

"Not your little problem. Your big problem. He can be your fake boyfriend this week."

"That's not a good idea."

"Why not? He's not dating anybody. Plus, he likes you. And he'll be alone this week while I'm with Mom."

"Because he's your dad. And you work for me. And I think that would be a little bit weird." Clover paused. "Wait. What do you mean he likes me?"

"I mean he likes you. Why wouldn't he like you? You're nice and you're a goddess."

"I'm dirt-encrusted on a daily basis," she said. She also lived in her jeans, fleece vests and turtlenecks, and any makeup she put on in the morning she'd sweated off by noon. Her blond hair never left its ponytail until night.

"So is Mother Nature."

"Is your father attracted to Mother Nature?"

"If he's smart he is. And he's smart, but don't tell him that. Come on, Clo, Pops thinks you're awesome for giving me this job. He says you're a good role model. He really does like you."

"Liking me is not the same as *liking* me. And even if he did like me, he's your father. I don't want things to be weird with you and me."

"You don't think it's already weird that you check him out every time he picks me up?"

Clover blushed crimson.

"i do not check your father out."

"I have lived all my life under the curse of the Sexy Single Dad. My own friends check him out. It's so gross. But it's not gross when you do it. It's adorable."

Clover glared at Ruthie across the office.

"Suit yourself," Ruthie said. "I didn't want a badass stepmother, anyway. I'll just write down the number for the male escort service. Do you like blond guys? Sven is half-off this week."

"Which half?"

"You'll have to call and find out…" Ruthie raised

her head and glanced out the window behind Clover's desk. "Speak of the devil. Pops is here. Time to fly."

Clover turned around and looked out at the truck pulling into the parking lot of Clover's Greenery, the finest plant nursery in the entire Mount Hood area according to PNW Garden Supply. That reputation was seemingly why they were ready to hand over a cool five million dollars to her for her two locations and the name. That was the sticking point. The name. It was her name. She kind of wanted to keep her name and use her name and sell plants with her name. Look at Erick, Ruthie's dad. Painted right on the side of his white Dodge Ram were the words Erick Fields—Cedar Roofing, Siding and Decking. He was his business. His name was his work. His work was his name. She respected that. Giving up her right to do business under the name Clover Greene would hurt. But would it hurt so much that five million dollars couldn't ease the pain?

Probably not.

She watched as Erick parked his truck and walked toward the office. He usually picked Ruthie up after work since Ruthie didn't have a car of her own, but today he was taking her to the airport to visit her mother for the week. Whether Clover wanted to admit it or not, Erick was cute and Clover was checking him out. Actually, *cute* wasn't the right word for Erick. He was handsome. Ruggedly handsome with his close-cropped brown-and-gray hair and his dark eyes that always seemed to be laughing at something. And tall? Definitely. And Erick was manly, with his buff-colored work coat, his steel-tipped work boots and his hands always stained with paint or deck stain. Manly without being macho, which she appreciated. She had no time for macho or swagger in a man. No posturing for her. Erick turned his head and looked through the window, raising his hand in a wave. Clover sat up straight. Oops. She got caught staring. She gave a quick casual wave back and spun around in her desk chair again, hoping Ruthie hadn't seen.

Ruthie was back at her small desk, clearing up her stuff and throwing it all into her backpack. It would be dull around here with Ruthie gone for the week and the nursery closed for winter after today. Clover always felt lost when she didn't have to come in to work at eight every morning and stay until eight every night. With the nursery taking up so much of her time, she didn't have much of a life outside it. When the nursery closed down for the season, Clover didn't know what to do with herself. Maybe her mother had a point. Maybe Clover should give her personal life more attention.

Or maybe that was her family talking, not her.

"You sure you don't want me to pimp you out to Pops?" Ruthie asked as she slung her backpack over her shoulder.

"As God is my witness, I do not want you to pimp me out to your father. Or anyone. Ever."

"Your loss. He can do magic with a Big Green Egg. That's not a sex thing, by the way. That's a grill."

"I know what a Big Green Egg is. I know it is not a sex thing."

"Although Mom does say Pops was good—"

"Stop right there, young lady. I have nothing but respect for your father. Especially since he puts up with you forty-five weeks out of the year. Now go. Have a great week with your mom. Don't worry about me."

"I'm going to worry about you, Clo."

"I'm your boss, I'm an adult and I'll be fine."

"You're my friend. You're a hot mess. You need help."

"I need a hug. Come here."

Ruthie groaned as Clover hugged her.

"No groaning. You'll have a great time in LA."

"Too much sun. I hate the sun," Ruthie said. "Why would I live here if I liked the sun?"

"I know you hate the sun. I'm sure it hates you, too. Wear sunscreen and a hat. You'll come back as ghastly pale and sickly looking as ever, I promise."

"You swear?"

"I swear."

"Good luck this week," Ruthie said, taking Clover by the arms. "Let me know what you decide about the nursery. I'd hate to lose my job here, but I'd also love to be friends with a millionaire, so whatever you choose, I'm on your side."

"Soon as I know, you'll know. Be safe."

"If I have to." Ruthie grabbed her jacket just as her father stuck his head through the office door.

"Hey, girls."

"Sexist," Ruthie said. "Try again."

"Hello, ladies?"

"Elitist." Ruthie pulled her jacket on and zipped it up. "One more try."

Erick dropped his chin to his chest, and Clover covered her mouth to stifle a laugh.

"Greetings, my fellow Americans," Erick said, his eyes rolled heavenward as if praying for patience.

"Better." Ruthie nodded her approval. "But only because we are Americans. You can't assume that about everyone."

"Are you ready to go, Ruthless? Please say yes."

"Ready," she said. "Just let me refill my water bottle real quick."

She walked out of the office with her water bottle in

hand, a normal errand but for the little wink she gave Clover as she walked past.

"How are you, Erick?" Clover asked, hoping that question didn't sound as awkward to his ears as it did to hers. Now that Ruthie had planted the idea in Clover's head of asking Erick out, she was having trouble making eye contact with him. And that was too bad. She really liked his eyes.

"I'm good. Ready for a few days off this week. You?"

"I hate days off," she said, sitting on top of her desk. "I'm about to get too many of them for my taste now that we're closed for the winter."

"Will you be climbing the walls by Tuesday?"

"No, but check on me again in late January when I've run out of busywork," Clover said. "Takes me a couple months to remember how to be lazy."

"It wouldn't take me nearly that long. But hey, thanks for giving Ruthie the whole week off. I know you could use the help cleaning up and locking things down."

"It's fine. She needs to see her mom and everything we have to do can wait until Ruthie gets back. I won't be in much this week, anyway. Gets too lonely around here when she's gone."

"Tell me about it. I'll be going nuts this week, too. Clean bathroom? No dishes in the sink? No bras hanging off the shower door? God, why doesn't my kid leave more often?"

"You know you'll miss me," Ruthie said from the doorway.

"I do?"

"You do," she said, punching him in the arm. "Come on, I'm ready as I'll ever be."

"You got everything?" Erick asked as he raised his

hand to tick items off on his fingers. "Meds. Phone. Charger. Your homework. Sunscreen."

"A Taser, a laser, a can of mace, an actual mace, a hunting knife, yes, yes, yes. I have everything I need for a week in LA. Let's go, Pops, we're going to be late."

"Bye, dear," Clover said. "Have fun or whatever it is that you do that's like having fun."

"Thanks, Clo. I left Sven's number on your desk."

"Sven?" Erick repeated as he grabbed Ruthie by her jacket collar and led her from the office. "Who's Sven?"

"Nobody," Ruthie said. "Just a male escort I hired for Clover."

"Is that in your job description?" he asked.

"Yeah, of course. What do you think I do here all day?"

"Your daughter is weird, Erick," Clover called after them, considering moving back into her desk nest.

"You don't have to tell me that. Have a good Thanksgiving," he said, gently force-marching Ruthie out to his truck.

"You, too," she said. After Erick and Ruthie had gone, Clover forced herself to reply to her two emails.

To the first—the five-million-dollar buyout offer she'd received from PNW Garden Supply's CFO—she replied with a simple I'll let you know on Monday. Happy Thanksgiving.

To her sister's email she replied with a smiley face emoji and a Great! Can't wait to see everyone!

She made sure to fill the email with unnecessary exclamation points to mask her incredible sense of dread about the whole shebang. All her family—her parents, two siblings, their spouses and seven kids under one roof for an entire day? There was not enough punctuation in the world to fake how much she was not looking forward to that.

Kelly replied to the email almost immediately.

Mom wants to know if we're going to be meeting anyone special on Thursday, Kelly wrote.

Clover picked up a trowel and considered stabbing her laptop with it so she wouldn't have to reply.

Instead she simply ignored the email and got to work cleaning. Potting soil and wheelbarrow went into the storage shed. Ferns back into the greenhouse. It wasn't the right time of year to trim a lemon tree so she moved it to the opposite corner of the office where it could spread out a little more until she could trim it down again to a more indoor-friendly size. And all the while she thought about what she would do with five million dollars and all the free time anybody could want.

Five million was a lot of money. Not enough to buy the world but plenty to go into her retirement account and leave enough to start a new company. But with the noncompete clause in the PNW Garden Supply offer, she wouldn't be able to start another nursery in Oregon. She could move to Northern California and open a nursery there. Then again, that's where her parents lived, which meant instead of hearing about how she needed to get married and have kids ASAP and STAT on major holidays, she'd hear it every single week.

Or she could stay in the Mount Hood area and open a landscaping business. Not quite as much fun as a nursery but it was still working with plants. Or she could take a few years off. Or she could move to Hawaii. Or Alaska. Or she could spend the money on male escorts for the next five years.

"You are not calling Sven," Clover said to herself. "Even if he is half-off this week."

Clover went to the sink and considered sticking her head under cold running water until she calmed down or drowned. Either would be preferable to her current confused, miserable and muddled state of mind. Instead she just washed all that potting soil off her hands with her lava soap and a nail brush. As she was drying her hands she saw headlights in the parking lot. After six already? She couldn't believe so much time had passed that it had gotten dark. She needed to head home and get to work cleaning her house. The deck needed to be cleaned off, too, in case the weather was clear enough to grill outside or use her fire pit for s'mores. Her nieces and nephews would make s'mores over that fire pit in the middle of a snowstorm if their parents would let them. She better get someone to fix the loose boards by the pit.

So much to do, so little desire to do any of it.

"Knock, knock."

Clover turned around and saw Erick sticking his head in through the workroom door.

"Oh, hey," she said, tossing her hand towel on the counter. "What's up?"

"My lovely brilliant wonderful daughter left her phone here. I have been commanded to fetch it and overnight it to her mom's house."

"Ruthie left her phone here? I thought she had that thing surgically attached to her hand."

"Yeah, me, too. And didn't I specifically ask her if she had her phone and her charger?"

"You did. Right after asking her if she had her meds."

"Okay. Glad I have a witness for this so I know it's one hundred percent her fault."

"All her fault," she said, trying not to laugh. Erick and Ruthie were hilarious together. Ruthie was comically sullen around her father, who was comically sullen around his daughter. They snarked at each other so well one would think sarcasm was the only language they both spoke. But it was impossible not to see how much Erick loved his girl and how much Ruthie adored her father, even if they did constantly harangue and harass each other. She called him "Pops," which he hated, and he called her "Ruthless," which she hated even more. Clover found it all endearing and entertaining. She wished she could tease her own parents like that.

"Ruthie said her phone's in her desk but she might have locked it in there."

"I'll get my key," Clover said. He followed her back into her office and Clover took the key off the wall hook. "You know, it is really not like her to leave her phone. She okay?"

"She's fine. She probably has it. She's probably pulling some kind of prank on me by sending me back here. There's a real possibility there's a snake in there," Erick said. "I know my daughter and she knows I hate snakes."

"I know her, too. So stand back. I'll protect you. Ready?" She stuck her key in the desk drawer lock.

"I hate snakes," Erick said.

"Set."

"Really hate snakes."

"Go." She opened the drawer and saw… "It's her phone."

"No snakes?" Erick had his eyes shut so tight it looked like he was in pain.

"No snakes. She actually forgot her phone. Wow."

"Maybe she is coming down with something. I hope she's not sick. You think this is a sign of a brain tumor or something?"

"She seemed fine today."

"Okay. I'll get going, then. According to Ruthie, I have to find a twenty-four-hour UPS store and demand they ship this to her overnight and the driver has to be hot, not normal hot—UPS-driver hot."

"That is a very specific request."

"Is Sven UPS-driver hot?" Erick asked as he stuffed the phone into his coat pocket.

"I have no idea what Sven looks like. Your daughter is trying to get me to hire a male escort this week because my family is coming to my house for Thanksgiving."

Erick lifted his chin and cocked an eyebrow.

"You all do Thanksgiving a little differently than most people."

Clover laughed. "Oh, no, we do it the traditional way. Too much food and tons of criticizing family members for their life choices."

"Who's the target?"

Clover pointed at herself. Erick barked a laugh.

"You? The target?"

"Me. The target."

"I don't buy it. Why you?"

"Why not me?" she asked.

"Because you own and operate your own business. You know more about plants than anyone in this entire state. You're respected by your employees, even my daughter, who doesn't respect anyone or anything, and you're...you know."

"What?"

"Easy on the eyes," he said.

"I am?"

"My eyes aren't complaining," he said. "Just saying,

my mom's always trying to get me to shave. She hates beards. But Ruthie won't let me shave it off."

"Why not?"

"One of her friends made the mistake of telling Ruthie her dad was 'hot.' Ruthie said I either had to grow a beard or wear a bag over my head."

"The beard was the right choice."

"But you don't have a beard from what I can tell." He narrowed his eyes at her face and Clover turned left and right, giving him a good look at her nonexistent beard. "Nope. No beard. No reason to pick on you for anything."

"They'll find a reason. They always do."

"I have a cousin in jail for bouncing checks, my grandfather's favorite hobby is sitting on his porch shooting his rifle at crows, and my aunt raises pygmy goats *inside* her house so, you know, your family should count their blessings."

"I'm thirty. I'm not married. I'm not dating anybody. I have no kids. I could have a billion dollars and be crowned Queen of the Mountain and that still wouldn't be enough for my family."

"Ah...that explains Sven." He nodded sagely.

"I'm about ready to hire him to play boyfriend for a week if it'll shut my family up about my biological clock for one day. Which reminds me—you free this week?"

"You asking me to be your Sven?"

Clover laughed. "No, I was actually asking you if you could fix my deck."

"Oh. Well, yeah. Sure. Big job?"

"Two loose boards and a broken slat."

"What color stain?"

"Clear. Homewares brand."

"I have some of that in my truck. I can come tomorrow morning, if it's not pouring."

"I'll write down my address for you," she said as she scribbled her home address on a note card and passed it to him. "I appreciate it. I have a fire pit and I know the kids will want to use it for marshmallows."

"I can get it all done in an hour. My treat."

"I pay people for the work they do. No freebies."

"You gave my daughter a job when nobody else would. I owe you."

"You don't owe me a thing. Ruthie's great at this job."

"I know she is, but she wouldn't have been great at her job if you hadn't taken a chance on her. Nobody wanted to give a sixteen-year-old girl with green hair, a horrible attitude and a criminal record a job except you. Not even McDonald's. Please. Let me fix your deck as a thank-you for keeping my kid out of trouble."

"Fine. Since it's only an hour's work. Then we'll call it even."

"Great. See you tomorrow morning around eight."

"Thanks, Erick. Have a good night in your empty house."

"You, too," he said. He started for the door and it was then that Clover realized that Ruthie was sneakier and more evil than she'd ever given the girl credit for. She'd left her phone here on purpose so Erick would have to come back for it and they'd be alone together. Clover would be angry except for one thing—she did really like Erick. And for that reason alone she said what she said.

"Hey, Erick?"

He turned back around in the doorway, and he did it so quickly it was as if he'd been hoping she'd say something to stop him.

"Yes, Clover?" he said in a playfully husky voice.

"I have something weird to ask you."

"You've met my child. You know I can handle weird. Ask it."

"Do you…would you…maybe would you want to be my Sven this week?"

2

ERICK STARED, SLIGHTLY slack-jawed, at Clover, who stared back, slightly sheepishly, at him. She was blushing, which he'd never seen her do before. It looked good on her, that blush. A little color in her pale cheeks. He'd thought more than once about the various ways of making her flush, blush and redden, but he hadn't considered this one. He should have.

"Are you offering to pay me to sleep with you?" he asked. "I hope so. That's been a fantasy all my life. I can go to a bar and you can come in and pick me up. We don't have to use real money. I'll accept Monopoly—"

"That is not what I'm asking."

"Bummer," he said. It was. He'd been nursing a crush on his daughter's boss for a good year now, ever since he met Clover the day Ruthie started working at the nursery. He hadn't done or said anything about the crush. Ruthie needed a job and a steady female presence in her life much more than he needed a girlfriend. But that fact had only stopped him from asking Clover out. It hadn't put a dent in his crush.

"Here's the thing," she said. "I could really use somebody to play boyfriend for Thanksgiving. That's all.

Somebody to deflect all those questions I get from my family about why I'm not married yet, when I'm getting married, when I'm having kids…"

"Can't you tell them to mind their own damn business?"

"You sound like Ruthie. Does it work when she tells you to mind your own damn business?"

"Well…no."

"See my problem? It would make everything so much easier if I had a date for Thanksgiving. I know you're alone this week. Ruthie told me. It's a free meal and you wouldn't have to be alone on the day. Interested?"

"Hmm…"

"Hmm…?"

"I kind of like being alone," he said. "Thanksgiving isn't a huge deal in my family. My grandmother's Coquille. She's always called Thanksgiving 'What exactly am I supposed to be thankful for?' Day."

"Yeah, can't blame her for that. Do you like free food?"

"I don't usually turn it down, but I don't drive out of my way for it."

"Okay," she said. "Just thought I'd ask."

"Wait. You're giving up on me already? That hurts."

"I'm not going to try to convince you to do something you don't want to do," Clover said.

"Why not?"

"Because no means no."

"I didn't say no."

"Then it's a yes?"

"I didn't say that, either. Come on. I'm a businessman. Let's haggle."

Clover laughed a nervous laugh, almost a giggle. She sat behind her desk and he sat on the desk next to her.

"You're pretty when you laugh," he said. "But you're also pretty when you don't laugh."

"You're sweet," she said. "I feel like I shouldn't have brought this up. I had a weak moment and your daughter set me up."

"She left her phone here on purpose, didn't she?" Erick asked.

"I am ninety-nine percent certain of it," Clover said.

Goddamn, she was pretty when she blushed. No doubt about it. Blue eyes, blond hair and the natural beauty of a woman too busy to bother wearing much makeup. She always sported lip gloss, though. An icy pale pink that gave her a sixties mod look. A kissable color like bubble gum. He wondered what she tasted like.

"That girl will do me in someday. I swear."

"She's just worried about me," Clover said. "It's sweet."

"I'm not used to my daughter being sweet. I'm more used to my daughter painting her bedroom walls and ceiling black, bribing an ex-con to give her a tattoo and flipping off the next door neighbor's cat."

"She flipped off the cat?"

"She said he was judging her."

"I think she's just trying to live up to her own reputation."

"It's working," he said. "So do you really need someone to play boyfriend for the week? It's that bad with your family?"

She sighed heavily and sat back.

"It's hard," she said. "They love me but that doesn't make the stuff they say easier to hear. They think they're saying, 'We love you and we want you to be happy,' but what I hear is, 'You're inadequate. you're a disappointment and you haven't done what you're supposed to do to make *us* happy.' They bug me so much about getting married that I'm scared to even date because I don't know if I'm dating to make them happy or dating to make me happy. I've almost signed up for Tinder ten times in the last year and talked myself out of it."

"I'd rather take a vow of celibacy than join Tinder. And I'm not even Catholic."

"Don't do that. That would be a waste."

He grinned at her and shrugged. "You think I'm cute?" he asked.

"You're hot," she said. "Like UPS-driver hot."

"That's hot."

"Smoking."

"This is fun," he said. "Why haven't we ever flirted with each other before?"

"Because your daughter works for me, and I didn't want to make it weird for her."

"Oh, yeah. Her. Kids are such cock blocks. That's the name of my parenting book if I ever write one, by the way."

"That bad?"

"I love my kid, but damn, she makes things complicated. I don't think I would have given asking you out a second thought if she was a normal kid. But this job was the miracle we needed. I didn't think anybody would give her a chance after the barn incident."

"Kids make stupid mistakes," she said. "We all did."

"At fifteen I snuck a couple beers from Dad's stash, 'borrowed' the car without permission and ran over the neighbor's bushes. I didn't commit ecoterrorism to protest factory farming."

"She's got principles. I'll give her that."

"She's got a criminal record for arson and destruction of private property is what she's got."

"That, too."

"You're good for her," Erick said. "This job's been good for her. I kept thinking about asking you out but then I thought Ruthie wouldn't want to work for you if we were dating. Or if we broke up."

"In this scenario we've already dated and broken up?" Clover asked.

"I'm a parent. We plan for all eventualities."

"I'm not a parent and I had the same thoughts—don't screw things up for Ruthie. But that's me being selfish. She's a great assistant. I'd hate to lose her."

"She's crazy about you. She needs a woman in her life. But her dad kind of does, too. Ask me what two hundred and sixty-eight means."

"What does two hundred and sixty-eight mean?"

"That's how many days until Ruthie starts college, and I have my house back. Not that I'm counting."

"Are you counting?"

"I'm counting."

"You know, my parents would probably be very impressed if they thought I were dating a single father. They'd think that was a ready-made family."

"You really want me to be your Sven?" Erick asked. He already planned on doing it. This woman had taken his angry petulant pyromaniac daughter and turned her into a functioning member of society in under a year. He'd do anything for this woman, including but not limited to pretending to be her boyfriend for a couple days.

"I would appreciate it," she said.

"We can have sex all week too, right?"

"Okay."

"What?" Erick burst into laughter.

"What?" she repeated. "Why are you laughing?"

"I didn't think you'd say yes. I was joking."

"You were?" Her blue eyes went wide.

"Well…yeah. I mean, not that I don't want to. I do want to. I swear to God, I thought you'd say no. I never guessed you'd say yes, not in a million years."

"And why not?" she asked as she crossed her arms over her chest. Oh, no, he'd put her on the defensive. Bad move.

"You're a little reserved."

"Reserved? Me?" She sat up straighter, prim as a schoolmarm.

"Your lowest cut shirt is a turtleneck."

"Is there something wrong with having a warm neck?"

"Not a damn thing. Obviously I misjudged you. I'm sorry," he said, not at all in the least sorry to discover Clover Greene wanted to sleep with him.

"Okay, I might be a little reserved," she said. "But it's not on purpose. When you own your own business and run it all by yourself, you tend to be all business."

"That's all I mean. I just never heard you talk much about a personal life. And Ruthie would have told me if you were dating anybody."

"No time," she said. "I guess that's why I said yes when you said…what you said."

"When I said I wanted to sleep with you?"

"Yes, that thing," Clover said. "I actually have time this week to do that sort of…thing. It's been a long time since I was involved with someone in a clothing optional type scenario."

"How long? Wait, don't answer that. That was a rude question."

"We're talking about sleeping together. It wasn't rude. It was a fair question."

"Okay, how long? I'll show you mine if you show me yours."

"You show me yours first."

"Years," he said. "A year and a half? About that. I was seeing someone right before Ruthie got arrested. Then my entire life turned into babysitting her every minute of the day. You?"

"I had a boyfriend for a few months about three years ago. We broke up when he moved to Seattle for work. My parents still ask about him."

"Ouch."

"I don't even miss him. They miss him."

Erick held out his hand and as soon as he did it, he wished he hadn't. His hands were a wreck—covered in deck stain with old scars and calluses. But she didn't seem to mind. She put her hand in his and he saw she, too, had scars and calluses on her hands.

"I need a manicure," she said. "My last manicure was about the same time as my last boyfriend."

"Never had a manicure," Erick said. "Never had a boyfriend, either. Ruthie tried to talk me into being gay because one of her girlfriends had a crush on me. I had to politely decline."

"This is nice. Holding hands. I'd forgotten how nice this was." Clover sat back in her chair again but didn't let his hand go.

"Very nice. I suppose it wouldn't kill me to be your Sven for the week."

"And if it's just through Thanksgiving, no big deal, right? Fake boyfriend, not real boyfriend."

"I could make you a very good fake boyfriend. I

can be fake nice, fake sweet, fake romantic. I can really fake it."

"I don't know if you could fake anything. You seem very genuine to me," she said.

"I'm good at faking being genuine. Have to be. Teenage girls see through bullshit like they have X-ray vision or something. Ruthie wouldn't have left her phone here if she didn't think you and I would actually like each other. She saw right through me. X-ray eyes."

"She didn't need X-ray eyes on me. Just normal eyes. I sort of kind of check you out occasionally when you come to pick her up."

"You do?"

"I do."

"For how long?"

"Um...since the first day you and Ruthie came by?" She winced. Erick tried very hard not to laugh at her extreme discomfort. Clover was seriously adorable, and he seriously adored her.

He put his hand on his cheek and batted his eyelashes. "Oh, no, you've set me to blushing."

"Stop it. I'm embarrassed enough as it is."

"Why?" he asked, letting her hand go.

"Well... I did sort of just accidentally agree to sleep with you."

"Nothing to blush over. I want to sleep with me, too. In fact, I do sleep with me every single night. I'm good in bed."

"Are you?"

"I sleep like the dead, eight straight hours every night."

"That isn't what I meant." She pointed at him through her hoodie pocket. "You are enjoying this."

"I haven't gotten laid in a long time. I would come

from a foot rub, I swear. Yes, I'm enjoying flirting with you. I'm a little out of practice, though. How am I doing?"

"Not bad. I'm enjoying this, too, and that's usually a good sign, right?"

"Definitely. Great sign."

"So…" she said, standing up and facing him. Her hands were still stuffed deep in her pockets. He knew she was thirty but with her hair in the ponytail and wearing jeans and a hoodie, she looked younger, fresh-faced and innocent almost. Or maybe it was the nervousness and the embarrassment that made her look so young. It was endearing, whatever the cause. He wanted to kiss her very much.

"So. You want to do this?" he asked.

"Tell me what 'this' is and I'll tell you if I want to do it."

"You need a boyfriend to shut your family up on Thanksgiving. I'd be happy to play that part. But I'd like to get to know you better first so it doesn't feel like we're faking it. If I could choose, I'd go home with you tonight."

"You want to sleep with me tonight? This night? Sunday night?"

"This very night," he said. "I also agreed to fix your deck at 8:00 a.m. and if I'm already there I can sleep later."

"Now I know why Ruthie punches you in the arm all the time."

He braced himself for an arm punch. Instead Clover rested her forehead on his shoulder and laughed softly. After two seconds her head was still there. He put one arm around her waist and pulled her a little closer to him. She didn't seem to mind that one bit so he wrapped his foot around her leg and pulled her even closer...

"Your shampoo smells good," he said. "Lemons?"

"That's not my hair. That's my office," she said, pointing up at the tree. "But you smell good."

"That's hard to believe."

"You smell like sweat and cedar. It's nice."

"We're like a couple of dogs sniffing each other," he said. "If this continues, my nose is going to end up in your crotch."

He felt her shaking with laughter against him. He heard the laughter, too, but that was normal. Feeling a woman laughing against him...it had been a long time since he'd felt that.

"Clover?"

"Yes?" She lifted her head and met his eyes. Their faces were only inches apart.

"How about I kiss you? And after I kiss you, then you can tell me where you think I should sleep tonight. What do you think about that?"

"I... I think that's a good idea," she said.

"Great. I'm going to kiss you now. You ready?"

"Ready as I'll ever be."

He leaned in and she raised her hand to stop him.

"What?" he asked, pulling back.

"I was trying to remember my breath situation. I had gum about an hour ago. I think I'm okay."

"You're okay, I promise. Now are you ready?"

"Ready now," she said. "Go for it."

"I'm going for it. Right now. This second." Except he wasn't because he remembered he hadn't kissed a woman on the mouth in over a year and he wondered if he'd forgotten how. To stall for time, he put his hands on Clover's waist and positioned her between his knees.

She put her hands on his shoulders and he wished he'd taken his coat off so he could feel her body heat better.

"Did you do it?" Clover asked. "I might have blinked and missed it."

"Hold your horses. I'm getting there. Just lining up my target. I want to make sure I don't miss. That would be embarr—"

Clover put her lips on his. Thank God one of them finally did it, he thought. But that's all she did, put her lips on his. She wasn't actually kissing him. She was leaning her mouth against his. He would have laughed but he didn't want to hurt her feelings. Nothing for it, he'd have to kiss her back.

He wrapped both arms around her and drew her against him. Slowly and softly he moved his mouth over her lips as he ran his hands up and down her back. Her lips were warm against his and full and tender and he wanted to bite them but decided to maybe wait on the biting until later. It wasn't an electric kiss but he did feel something warm in the pit of his stomach and that warmth was getting warmer with every passing second. Clover opened her mouth.

Not warm.

Hot.

Very hot…

He slipped his tongue gently between her lips and Clover murmured a sweet sensual sound of pleasure and approval. He kissed her a little harder, pulled her a little closer. Her hands moved from his shoulders to the back of his neck. Good sign. She wanted to touch him. And he definitely wanted to touch her. What was with this damn hoodie? Was it made of wool? He couldn't even feel her heat through it. Stupid sensible wardrobe. He wanted this woman naked or at least in a T-shirt.

He gave a little sigh of frustration and Clover pulled back from the kiss.

"Did I do something wrong?" she asked, wide-eyed.

"Yes."

"What?"

"You put on appropriate fall clothing this morning. Why did you do such a thing?"

"It's fall."

"No excuse."

She rolled her eyes.

"You're already trying to get me naked?" she asked.

"Not naked. Just less clothed. Can we get rid of this hoodie? I can't even feel your bra strap through it."

"You're the one wearing the big coat."

"I can take my coat off. I can take off anything you want if it'll get you to kiss me again."

"You liked it?" she asked.

He nodded. Vigorously.

She smiled, her skin pinking again. God, she was pretty.

"I liked it, too. A lot. A whole lot."

"Enough to invite me home tonight?"

"If we do…does that mean you'll expect, you know."

"Sex?"

"That."

"No. I'm not going to expect sex from a woman too nervous to say the word *sex* to me."

"Sex. Sex, sex, sex. I'm not nervous. I'm just…"

"What?"

"Nervous. Yes. You got me. I am nervous. I feel like I know you really well because of Ruthie and everything she's told me about you. But you and I don't actually know each other that well because…"

"Of Ruthie. I know. I get it," he said. "I would like

to get to know you a lot better. Especially if it means more kissing. Et cetera."

"Do you want to spend the night at my house? I won't guarantee there'll be more than kissing but there'll definitely be kissing. And lots of it."

"I'd like that," he said. "I would like that very much." He took her hand in his and squeezed it. Her hand trembled. She really was nervous. More reason to spend as much time together as possible. Nobody would believe they were a real couple if she was this nervous around him.

"Okay. You have my address in your pocket. I'll head home and you come by whenever you're ready. You know, after you find a twenty-four-hour UPS store."

"Ruthless will have to wait for her phone until Tuesday. Serves her right for setting her old man up."

"You're not an old man. You're only thirty-eight, right?"

"Yeah, but in parent-of-a-teenager years, I'm ninety-eight."

"You look great for your age."

"You look great, period." He stroked her cheek with the back of his hand. It was the only part of his hand soft enough to touch a soft part of her.

"You're too good at making me blush," she said. "I hate being so pale."

"It's fun. I can see when I'm getting to you. It's like an indicator light."

"I think my indicator light says, 'Engine needs servicing.'"

"God, I'd love to service your engine."

She groaned in horrified amusement.

"I don't even know what that means," he said, "but I'm pretty sure it was dirty."

"I kind of hope it was," she said.

"Can I sleep in your bed with you tonight?" he asked. "No sex necessary. Just sleep. I'd like to get comfortable with you."

"I would…yeah. I would like that, too."

"Great. I'll be right over after I get some stuff at my house. An hour. No later."

He hopped off the desk and walked to the door.

"Erick?" Clover said.

"Yeah?"

She walked over to him and put her hand on the back of his neck again. She was a good height, perfect height for kissing while standing, which he discovered when she kissed him once more.

"Okay," he said when she stepped back.

"Okay, what?"

"Okay, I won't be over in an hour. I'll be over in *half* an hour."

"Don't rush," she said. "I want to take a shower and change the sheets on the bed."

"Take your time." He kissed her on the cheek and went to leave again. But he stopped and looked back at her.

"Ruthie and I drive each other crazy but she's my daughter and she's the best thing that ever happened to me. She doesn't need to know all the dirty details about her father's personal life, but I wouldn't feel right keeping this a secret from her. It would really hurt her if I didn't tell her something."

"You're absolutely right. She may act like she's thirty-seven, but she is still seventeen. She should hear it from you."

"I'll call it a date. Can we call it a date?"

"Yes, you can call it a date."

"I'm glad she forgot her phone," he said, putting "forgot" into quotes.

"She's a smart girl."

"Sexist," Erick said.

"She's a smart fellow American," Clover said, laughing. "Even if she can't mind her own business."

"Better me than Sven," Erick said. "I'll give your money back at the end of the week if you're not satisfied."

"Sounds like a very good deal especially since I'm not paying you."

He zipped up his coat and patted his pocket to make sure Ruthie's phone and Clover's address were still there. "You need me to pick up anything before I come over?" he asked. "Food? Wine? Whips? Chains? Condoms?"

"I'm on the pill," she said. "Heavy periods. Sorry. TMI."

"I have a teenage daughter. You're going to have to do better than heavy periods to TMI me. And I'm buying condoms, anyway. Not because we have to use them. Just because I want someone to know I might be getting laid this week."

"I'm allergic to latex."

"It's okay. I'm so clean it's depressing."

"We'll talk about it. Later. We're just sleeping tonight. Right?"

"Right. Just sleeping. And kissing."

"That, too."

He started to leave.

"But maybe more than kissing," she said.

He didn't answer. He just walked out the door before he walked back to her and kissed her for a good three or four hours. Soon as he was in the cold night air on the way to his truck he pulled his own phone out of his pocket and sent a text message to Candace, his ex-wife.

Give your daughter a message for me, he wrote. Tell her she's in trouble.

For what? Candace wrote back. She should know better by now than to ask that question.

She'll know what I mean.

I'll tell her. Anything else?

Yeah, Erick wrote. Tell her thank you.

3

DON'T PANIC, CLOVER told herself. Then she told herself that again. It wasn't working. She was panicking.

She stood in the middle of her living room and glanced around at her house. No denying, she had a cute house. Not big. Perfect size for a woman who lived alone. Living room, office and kitchen downstairs. Master bedroom and guest bedroom upstairs. Half bath by the kitchen. Full bath by the master. Bamboo floors covered in woven rugs. Walls painted a rustic red downstairs and a pretty lake blue upstairs. Plants were everywhere, of course—ferns, ficus and flowers. She hoped Erick wasn't allergic to flowers. This slumber party would be over before it started if he was. Ruthie had worked for her nearly a year and Erick picked his daughter up all the time. Had she ever seen him sneeze around the plants? Not that she recalled, but then again that would be a really bizarre thing to remember. She was freaking out and she knew it.

"Calm down, Clover," she told herself.

"I am calm," she said but she knew she wasn't. She hadn't been expecting company tonight. Certainly not tall, handsome, male company. She was torn between excitement and panic.

"Priorities, Clover. First things first. Man coming over…spending the night. What do I do? Clean stuff. What stuff? All the stuff."

She'd fallen asleep on the sofa last night reading and the throw pillows and blankets were still a mess. She straightened the pillows and folded the blanket neatly. But it was a throw blanket and didn't look right in a neat rectangle so she tossed it over the back instead. It ended up looking nearly identical to how it looked before but at least it was purposefully messy and not accidentally messy.

All the dishes in the kitchen sink she crammed into the dishwasher and started it running. She put the basket of her yet-to-be-folded socks and underwear in the laundry room, draping a clean towel over the piles of panties on top. She dug through the linen closet upstairs for clean sheets. Currently on her bed was red and blue flannel. She liked a cold house to sleep in at night with warm blankets piled high. Sometimes she even slept with the window cracked to let in the cold night air. She lived near Lost Lake and the air was as clean and fresh as anyone could ever want, and it seemed a shame to not have some of that crisp clean air in her house. If she remembered correctly, men tended to be warmer than women. Maybe no flannel sheets, then. She found her summer sheets, plain blue cotton, and stripped the white-and-blue-checkered quilt off her bed. She replaced the sheets and fluffed the pillows. Then she had to decide—did she want to remake the bed? Hadn't she already told Erick she had to change the sheets? Would he think she was some kind of freak if she made the bed all of an hour before unmaking it to sleep? Was she overthinking this? Yes, she was over-thinking this.

"You're overthinking this, Clover. Stop it."

She stopped it and just made the bed, anyway. She liked made beds. The room looked more inviting when the bed was made. On the bedside table was a little milk glass lamp that she switched on, flooding the room with low gentle light. Clover stepped back and took in the effect. Nice. Her small bedroom looked almost... romantic? Like a room at a cozy inn. Rustic but pretty.

What else? Bathroom. Oh, yeah, she better clean the bathroom. Erick had said with Ruthie gone he looked forward to using a clean bathroom all week. Clover wiped down the sink and the tile counter, wiped the toothpaste spots off the mirror, opened the drawer and slid into it everything from the counter. When that was done she heaved a sigh of relief. Then she saw herself in the mirror.

While frantically cleaning, she'd gotten a little sweaty and her hair was matted down on her forehead and what little of her makeup she'd still been wearing when she'd arrived home half an hour ago was now gone. She undressed fast and hopped into the shower. That morning she'd washed her hair so she didn't do that again but she managed to soap up and shave her legs in a record time of seven minutes. Wearing only her towel, she brushed her hair again and pulled it into a neat ponytail. She put on a fresh coat of mascara and lip gloss and found her nicest pair of normal underwear—white cotton boy shorts—and put those on. The question was, what to wear over them. Put on her jeans again? She had some cute Christmas paja-mas somewhere—shorts and a tank top—but it wasn't even Thanksgiving yet. And those did show a lot of skin. She didn't want Erick to think she was trying to seduce him. She wasn't. Was she? No, of course not. They'd already talked about it. No sex tonight. Just a sleepover. Of course then he'd joked about buying condoms and she'd told him about her latex allergy, which sort of kind of maybe made it sound like she did want to have sex with him. Or maybe—

"Stop it, Clover. You're thirty, not fifteen." Truth. But she felt nervous as a teenager for some reason. She knew the reason. She hadn't told Erick the reason but she would. Or maybe not. She'd simply tell him she was out of practice.

"Now you are acting like a kid," she told herself. "Grow up."

Clover pulled a nightgown from off a hanger in the back of her closet. This was what she wore on the coldest nights, ankle-length with full sleeves. A very pretty nightgown if somewhat old-fashioned. Maybe too old-fashioned? The doorbell rang. Too late to change. Clover threw on her pale yellow bathrobe and walked down the steps to the front door. Erick stood on her front porch with a black gym duffel bag over his shoulder and a smile on his face.

"Nice house," he said as she let him in. "Didn't know you lived on Lost Lake. You like it out here?

"Love it," she said. "Did you have trouble finding it? The roads can be a little winding."

"A little?" He dropped his duffel on the floor by the door and started untying the laces on his work boots. "I swear David Bowie wearing a giant codpiece gave me directions, that's how winding they are."

"Never figured you for a *Labyrinth* fan. Isn't that kind of a girl movie?" she teased.

"It's a Ruthie movie, which means I've seen it

approximately…" He yanked one boot off. "One million…" He yanked the second boot off. "One hundred thousand…" He pulled his coat off. "Times."

He hung his coat on the coatrack and turned to look her in the face. Not knowing what else to do she just stood there with her hands in her robe pockets trying to look casual when she felt anything but.

"Did you really get lost finding the house?" she asked, feeling bad she hadn't given him better directions.

"Nah. I was just out here last month putting cedar siding on one of the new Lost Lake rental houses. I know these roads pretty well."

"That cedar cabin down the road?" she asked.

"That's the one. Chris Steffensen hired me to do the job. Although I think I did too good of a job. He and his girlfriend are living in it now. They were supposed to rent it out."

"It did turn out great. I came this close to offering to buy it from him."

"Why? This place is great."

"Feels too big, I guess," she said. "You know, since I live alone and…"

"Hold still," he said.

"Why?"

"I'm going to kiss you before we get weird and awkward around each other. You good with that?" he asked. She was already feeling both weird and awkward so she was glad he mentioned it.

"Oh. Okay. Good idea."

"Also I'm going to kiss you because I want to kiss you."

"Even better idea."

He put his hands on her waist and she placed hers on

his shoulders. She imagined they looked like models on a How to Kiss Like Reasonable Adults public service poster. This was easily the strangest fake relationship she'd ever been in.

But.

Strange as it was, as soon as Erick's lips met hers and she relaxed enough to enjoy the kiss, well...she enjoyed the kiss. He tasted like toothpaste, which made her smile against his mouth. She'd brushed her teeth, too, in anticipation of more and deeper kissing. And the more and deeper he kissed, the more and deeper she wanted him to kiss her. Erick knew how to kiss. He could teach classes on it. She hoped she was making the grade. When he stepped closer and slid his hands from her waist to the back of her neck and the curve of her hip, she had a feeling she was at least passing this test.

"Well..." he said against her lips. "What do you think? Still weird and awkward?"

"Yes," she admitted. "But less weird and awkward now."

"Hmm...a little kissing made it a little less weird. You think a lot of kissing will make it a lot less weird?"

"Stands to reason," she said. "I mean, if you run the numbers, that adds up."

"So we should probably kiss some more, right?"

"We should. Definitely."

"Definitely, she says. I like a definite woman." He reached for her again but she stepped back, suddenly awkward again. She couldn't get over thinking that this was Ruthie's dad. Ruthie's insanely sexy dad. Why did Ruthie have such a sexy dad? Work was going to be weird as heck next week.

"Let me show you around the house first," she said.

"You know, since you're supposed to be my boyfriend, you should probably know where the bathroom is."

"For a lot of reasons."

She showed him the living room and he admired the layout and the finish on her bamboo floors. In the kitchen he admired her box window. She would have showed him the deck but it was already pitch-black out and raining. That could wait until tomorrow. He liked the bathroom for the paint color and the nice fixtures. He actually said that—"nice fixtures."

"No one has complimented my fixtures before," she said. "This is new."

"I like a lady who knows how to pick a faucet."

"Chrome is so dated," she said. "Copper is classic."

"You are speaking my language. What's upstairs?" he asked. His question sounded so innocent but something in his eyes looked quite devilish. She liked devilish.

"Oh, another bathroom. Guest room. My bedroom."

"You have copper fixtures upstairs, too?" he asked.

"Of course. I designed the whole place myself."

"I wouldn't mind seeing the upstairs. You know, for the fixtures," he said.

"Right. The fixtures."

Clover took him up the steps—which he also admired for the fine grain of the cedar—and showed him her bathroom. He approved. She showed him the guest room. He also approved of that.

"And here's my room," she said. "Kind of a small bed. Hope that's okay. I can sleep in the guest—"

Erick had walked to the bed while she was chatting away nervously and before she could get any more words out he'd turned around and fallen onto the bed on his back.

Her full-size bed suddenly looked like a twin with Erick on it. He wallowed a little on the quilt, rolled left and rolled right, bounced once or twice, then sat up on his elbows and looked at her. She liked the look he gave her.

"Comfy," he said.

"Good. As I was saying…you're sort of, you know, big—"

"Who have you been talking to?"

"Stop. You know what I mean. You are tall and this is a small bed."

"I like small beds. You can't hide from me in this bed."

She tucked a strand of hair that didn't actually exist behind her ear.

"What makes you think I want to hide from you?"

"You're wearing a bathrobe over a nightgown that's got so much material to it I could make a schooner sail out of it. And you're doing that grandma thing where you're holding the lapels of your robe together like you're afraid I'll see your neck or some other unmentionable part of your body. It's very cute, this shyness."

"I really want to be sexy and flirty with you, but if I ever knew how to do that, I've forgotten how."

"You are sexy."

"Not like you are."

He raised his eyebrows.

"How am I sexy?" he asked. "And please, be specific."

"You're very comfortable with yourself. I like that. I'm not as comfortable with myself."

"You're comfortable with yourself at work."

"I am, but this isn't work. And I don't know you very

well. Even though I know you really well. That made more sense in my head, I promise."

"You know me as Ruthie's dad. That's how you know me, and as dear old dad, you do know me well. Ruthie's in LA right now and it's just you and me. Now you get to know the other side of me that has absolutely nothing to do with my daughter even though it's the reason she exists."

"I want to get to know that side of you. I want to get to know that side of me, too. But you know how it is, running your own business."

"Mine's nothing like yours. I can pick my jobs, tell people no if they try to book me on a day I need to be at Ruthie's school or something. Your place is open seven days a week, eight to eight, and I've never once gone there to drop off Ruthie or pick her up and not seen you there with your nose in a stack of invoices or with a trowel, a hose and a pair of hedge clippers in your hand. You work your ass off."

"It's still there. I think." She patted her backside. "Yup. I don't work that hard."

"How long have you lived in this house?"

"Um, two years and six months," she said.

"Where is everything?"

"What?"

"Where is everything? You have furniture and you have plants. I saw two books downstairs and those were on gardening. No art on the walls, no pets, no souvenirs from vacations anywhere. This place looks like a bed-and-breakfast. A nice bed-and-breakfast but not a home."

"I'm not here very often."

"Your office looks more like home than your home."

"It is my home."

"And that's my point." He sat up on the edge of the bed. "Your office is lived-in. It's homey. You have pictures of your family on your desk and a stuffed puppy or something—"

"That is a sock monkey. A pink sock monkey and his name is Alejandro. Your daughter gave him to me."

"Of course she did. You have a messy office. It looks like someone's home. This house looks like you bought it yesterday turnkey and just brought a suitcase of clothes with you. Do you even have anything in your nightstand? A book? Chapstick? Vibrator?"

She narrowed her eyes at him. He narrowed his eyes at her. Then he reached out and opened the nightstand drawer.

"I knew it," he said. "Nothing."

"Not nothing. There's something in there, right?"

"Yeah. A packet of silica gel that the manufacturer put in here that you never took out. Oh, and this is the receipt for your lamp."

She snatched both of them out of his hand and tossed them into the white wicker trash can.

"Okay, so I'm not home much," she said. "Don't you start in on me, too. I get this from my parents."

"Whoa there." He raised both hands in surrender. "I'm not telling you that you need to get married and have kids. I've been married. I've had a kid. Trust me, neither one is a requirement for happiness. I would die for my daughter. I've also come close to killing her a few times. Marriage and kids is another kind of work. What I'm saying is it looks to me like you need to work less, not more. At least for this week. Maybe be a homebody. Maybe be…my body?"

She put her hands on her hips and stared him down.

"You're sexy when you glare at me like that," he said.

"I am not. You just said I'm wearing a robe over a schooner sail."

"You're still sexy."

"I don't feel sexy," she said, crossing her arms over her chest again.

"How do you feel?"

"Prudish. Uncomfortable."

"Well, you aren't prudish. You asked me to spend the night with you."

"I think that was your idea."

"Beside the point. You liked the idea."

"I did. Kind of." She smiled.

"But what about this uncomfortable thing? Are you uncomfortable with me? Or are you uncomfortable with you?"

"What do you mean?"

"You said you liked that I'm comfortable with myself. Are you comfortable with yourself?"

"If I were, do you think I'd be wearing a schooner sail?"

"Good point. Maybe let's lose that. Can we?"

"You're trying to get me naked already? That was fast."

"Not naked. Not yet, anyway. Here." He stood up in front of her and unzipped his black fleece Columbia jacket. Under it he wore a white V-neck T-shirt. He tossed the Columbia jacket onto the back of her armchair and then pulled the T-shirt off over his head. "Take this."

"What?" She looked at his naked chest in shock. Shock, surprise and pleasure.

"I want you to put on my T-shirt. If you would. If you wouldn't mind. I'd appreciate it. You're really doing me a favor here."

"Doing you a favor by putting on your T-shirt," she repeated.

"When a beautiful woman puts on my shirt, it makes me feel better about the state of the world. And if the only other thing she has on is her underwear, I'm downright optimistic for the future. And don't we all need a little more optimism these days?"

"So I put on your T-shirt and traipse around in my underwear and you'll feel better about world events?"

"Now that you mention it, I don't really know exactly what traipsing is. But I would like you to do it, yes. Whatever it is."

"So you'll feel better about the world?"

"Right," he said, nodding. "I'm feeling perkier already."

"Perky...that's what we're calling it now, are we?"

"Lose the sail and I'll be downright cheerful."

She sighed and took the T-shirt out of his hands. She tried not to stare at his chest as she did it, but she didn't try very hard. He had a good chest, nice broad shoulders and the right amount of chest hair—more than a boy's and less than a Sasquatch's. Flat stomach, which was good. No washboard, which was better. She would feel really uncomfortable getting undressed in front of a man with a six-pack. She much preferred normal bodies over perfect bodies considering just how unperfect her body was.

"I'll go change in the bathroom. If that's okay," she said.

"Your pony, your saddle. You change where you want. I'll be right here." He patted the bed.

She walked into the bathroom and shut the door behind her. She went to lay Erick's T-shirt on the bathroom counter but she paused and lifted it to her nose.

Cedar. Cedar and soap. She would happily smell that all
night. Maybe she could, too, if she didn't screw this up.

"Clover?" Erick called out, and she almost dropped
the shirt on the floor.

"Yes?"

"You mind if I open the window a little? I like night
air."

She smiled and pressed the shirt to her chest.

"Me, too," she said. "Go for it."

"Plus if you're cold you'll have to come to me for
body heat," he said, and she quietly laughed to herself.
This was flirting. Good flirting. The man could really
flirt. So could she, couldn't she?

"Or I could just get the extra blankets out of the
closet," she called back through the door. Her robe was
gone and now the gown.

"Where's the linen closet?" he replied as she pulled
his T-shirt on over her head.

"In the hall. Why?"

"I'm just going to go throw all your blankets out in
the backyard. Be right back."

She didn't believe him until she felt his footsteps on
the floor and heard a door opening and closing.

"Oh, don't you dare," she said as she walked out
of the bathroom to find Erick nowhere near her linen
closet. He was on her bed. No. Not on. In her bed. He
was in her bed and his pants weren't. She knew his
pants weren't in the bed because they were on the floor
at her feet.

"Kidding," he said.

"I knew you were."

"Good. Very good. Great even."

"That I knew you were kidding?"

"That you're standing in the middle of the bedroom in your underwear," he said.

"Yeah, I guess I am." She looked down at bare legs, her bare feet and the T-shirt barely covering anything past her hips. "You feeling better about world events yet?"

"Life is good. Very good. Could be better."

"How so?"

"If instead of there..." He pointed at her feet on the floor. "You were here." He tapped the pillow next to him.

"Well... I wouldn't want you to lose your sunny outlook on life," she said. He looked so inviting in her bed, warm and strong and male and everything she'd wanted for a long time. She slipped in next to him and lay on her back, her head on the pillow.

"Comfortable?" he asked as he rolled onto his side and propped himself up on one arm.

"Very." She turned her head to look at him and found his face only inches from hers.

"Are you?"

"I am," she said. "Your shirt's nice."

"Cotton. Preshrunk. I go for the fancy shit."

"I might keep it."

"I'd like that." He raised his hand to her face and traced her lips with his fingertips. "Although if you decided at some point tonight that you hated it and wanted to burn it, I wouldn't complain about that, either."

"I don't think that's likely."

"No?"

"Why burn it? I'd use it for washing my car."

He nodded, grinning his cocky half grin. "Good idea."

"Harrison Ford."

"What? Where?" Erick glanced around the room.

"No, you. I was trying to figure out earlier who you reminded me of. You look like a young Harrison Ford. But with a beard."

He lowered his head so that their lips were barely an inch apart and whispered two words to her.

"I know."

4

CLOVER STARTED TO laugh but his kiss put a stop to that nonsense. At first the kiss was gentle, nothing but his mouth moving over hers as he explored her top lip with his lips and her bottom lip with his teeth. She felt ridiculous just lying there with her hands gripping the sheets at her sides, so she forced her fingers to uncurl and placed her hands on his shoulders and back. He had such warm, smooth skin that once she touched him with her bare hands she couldn't stop. His tongue slipped between her teeth and she slid her palms down his long back and up again. The knots of nervousness that had knit up her entire body since Erick rang her doorbell slowly started to loosen. She should do this more often. Like…every night of her life.

Erick pressed closer to her. She felt his long, hairy legs against her not-quite-as-long and thankfully much-less-hairy ones. She ran her bare foot up the back of his calf as he kissed her along her jawline and all the way down to her neck.

"You feel good," he said into her ear.

"I do feel good," she said.

"You feel good to me."

"I knew what you meant." She smiled up at him. "Just saying, I'm feeling better."

"Good." He smiled down at her. "I want to make you feel good. You look really sexy in my shirt and on your back."

"Thank you," she said. "I'm feeling sexy…ish."

"Let's try this." He gently lifted her head and pulled her ponytail holder out of her hair. She'd meant to do that earlier in the bathroom and had forgotten. He tossed the elastic onto the nightstand and ran his fingers through her hair, massaging her scalp lightly and smoothing her hair down her back.

"Very nice," he said. "First time I've ever seen you with your hair down."

"I'd hate to get it caught in a wood chipper," she said.

"I like that you wear it up all the time. Makes seeing it down much more interesting."

"My hair is interesting?"

"You are interesting," he said. "Very, very interesting. I'm going to figure you out."

"Not much to figure out."

"Oh, there has to be something mysterious here. How could a woman who is so beautiful have no idea how beautiful she is? I'll think about that tomorrow. Right now I'm thinking about this."

He kissed her and she opened up for him without hesitation. She loved the way he kissed her. It was sensual, yes. Sensual and warm and slow. But tender, too. She hadn't expected the tenderness in his kiss. Or maybe it wasn't him. Maybe she was feeling all the tenderness. He had called her beautiful and sexy and those words were like aloe on a sunburn, instantly taking the sting out of a throbbing wound.

Clover tensed as Erick shifted his body so that he

was half on the bed and half on top of her. She could feel his erection pressing against her thigh through the black boxer briefs he wore. She tried to ignore it as he kept kissing her but it was so hard and insistent and right there. Her heart beat wildly in her chest, in her neck, in her throat. She had forgotten how intense kissing could be, how terrifying in the best sort of way. She felt panicky, aroused, excited, eager, but didn't know how to tell Erick that in words. She let her body do the talking. She carefully moved her thigh, letting it graze against the hardness pressed against her.

"Minx," he said, and laughed softly. "I was hoping you hadn't noticed that."

"Hard not to notice it," she said against his lips. "Very, very hard…"

She raised her head to kiss him again and he stopped her with a question.

"Do you want to touch me?" he asked.

"I am touching you." Her hands were on his shoulders. He lowered his chin and narrowed his eyes. "Oh… you want me to touch it."

"No. I asked if you wanted to touch me. I didn't say you could. I'm asking if you want to. So… Clover Greene, do you want to touch me?"

"I do," she said. "But—"

"You can also touch my butt, yes."

She giggled and the sound surprised her. She sounded so young, so nervous.

"How is it you're only eight years older than me?" she asked.

"Well, you were born in 1985 and I was born in 197—"

"I feel like a kid around you. That's what I'm saying. And you know it."

"You have a kid at twenty-one, you grow up fast. When did you start your company?"

"Five years ago."

"I started mine sixteen years ago. Why did you start yours?"

"My grandparents sold their old vacation house and split the money with the grandkids. It was enough to start the nursery. You?"

"I had a one-year-old daughter, a wife with a drinking problem and we lived in a trailer with no heat. It was either work my ass off or freeze my ass off."

"I...I didn't know that about your ex. I'm sorry. Ruthie never told me."

"Ruthie's mom sobered up a long time ago. Ruthie doesn't know how bad it was. She doesn't need to know."

"You had to grow up faster than I did," she said. "I guess that's why you seem so together."

"Hey, I had to work and make money. Had no choice," he said. "You had a choice. How much did your grandparents give you?"

"A hundred thousand dollars."

He whistled. "How many people get a windfall like that and start a business with it? Maybe one out of a hundred? One out of a thousand? Everyone else would have spent it on cars or a house or socked it away for retirement. Instead you built a business with it, a business you work at twelve hours a day and seven days a week. You didn't have to work as hard as you did, but you did it, anyway. That's much more impressive than working because you have to."

"I don't know about that."

"I know about it," he said, stroking her cheek. "I'm older and wiser, right?"

"I didn't say you were wise."

"It was implied."

"You make me feel young," she said. "That's all. In the good way. In the 'nervous to be making out with a guy' way."

"That's a good way to be nervous. But I'd rather you be relaxed than nervous. I don't want to scare you."

"You don't." She shook her head. "It's not fear. It's… excitement."

"No, this is excitement." He pressed his erection into her thigh again. She inhaled sharply and clung tighter to his shoulders.

"Yes," she said.

"Yes, what?"

"Yes, I want to touch you very much. Can I, please?"

"That's the politest way any woman has ever asked to rub my cock in my life. Your manners are impeccable, Ms. Greene."

"My parents raised a lady."

"Does that mean you'll stick your pinky out while you're stroking me off?"

"Probably."

"This I've gotta see."

Erick rolled onto his back and underneath the covers pulled off his underwear and tossed it across the room. He lay flat on his back with his hands behind his head…waiting.

"O…kay…" she said. "You are naked in my bed."

"I can put my watch back on if you want."

"No. Naked is good. But can I turn off the light?"

"If it makes you feel better."

"It would."

She switched off the lamp and slowly scooted across

the sheets toward him. He put one arm around her back and slid even closer to her.

Without saying another word, he kissed her. It was a deep, long, sensual kiss, much deeper and harder than he'd kissed her before. With the lights off, everything seemed to mean more, to matter more. They were no longer playing. And Erick was naked, completely, not even wearing that smile. She took a ragged breath as she placed her hand on the center of his chest. It pleased her to feel how hard his heart beat against her hand. He was nervous/scared/excited, too.

Tentatively she slid her hand down his chest to his stomach and stopped there while he kissed her neck under her ear.

"Take your time," he whispered. "I have all night."

"Thanks for being understanding," she said.

"I don't know why you're so nervous with me but it doesn't matter. You set the pace. I'm just happy to be here."

"Are you? Happy, I mean?"

"As happy as I've been in a long time."

Clover slipped her hand under the sheet and wrapped it around his erection. Erick took a quick breath in.

"Okay," he said. "Now I'm happy."

She smiled but didn't say anything. She wanted to concentrate on the task at hand. The very pleasant task at hand. Gently she ran her hand over the length of him a few times just to get the feel of him. He was incredibly hard from base to tip, so hard she felt his cock pulsing against her palm. He was big, not huge but definitely a good size. She imagined putting it inside her and knew it would fill her and stretch her and she'd love every inch of it. But not yet. She wasn't ready for that yet. Was she? If they had sex he'd probably want her to take all her clothes off and that would be awkward. But maybe not. But probably so. She was overthinking it again and forced herself to concentrate only on Erick's beautiful body and forget about hers.

She squeezed him lightly and watched his face to see what happened. He must have liked it because his head fell back and his throat jumped like he'd had to take a quick breath or swallow hard. Even in the dark she could see his lips were slightly parted and she could hear him panting as she stroked him, lightly at first but then harder as it became clear to her he liked what she was doing. Down and up and down and up...she slid her hand down and up him again and again. Erick reached over his head and gripped her headboard with one large hand. He moved his hips with her hand, lifting them as she stroked downward and pulling back when she stroked up. It was obscene, watching him move like that, like he was fucking her hand. He was fucking her hand and she could tell he would come soon if she didn't stop. She had no intention of stopping.

"You should maybe stop," Erick said, and his voice was tight and hoarse, like it hurt to talk.

"Why?" she asked, her hand still on him but no longer moving.

"When I get close to coming I say really inappropriate things. And you're getting me there."

"Inappropriate how? We're in bed together. Unless you start spitting out math formulas or threatening to assassinate world leaders, I don't know what you'd say that would be inappropriate."

"I have a very dirty mouth. You don't know how dirty."

"Can I find out how dirty? Now you've got me curious."

"Okay, but don't say I didn't warn you."

"You warned me," she said. "Can I keep going now?"

"God, yes, and please and thank you. But lick your hand first. Wet helps."

"Lick my hand?"

"See? It's already happening."

"I've never licked my own hand before," she said as she licked her palm. "I mean, unless there was chocolate on it."

"Maybe next time."

She felt more confident this time when she wrapped her fingers around him. Clover had no doubt in her mind at all he was enjoying himself and, more specifically, enjoying her as she enjoyed him. She started slow again, massaging him and working her way up the shaft and down to the base with a firm grip. As she slid her hand up again she pulled him very gently and he let out a soft groan from the back of his throat.

"Fuck, that feels good… I want to pound your pussy so hard you can't walk tomorrow."

"Wow," she said, blinking. "You weren't kidding."

"It just comes out," he said. "Sorry."

"Don't say you're sorry. It was…sexy. Intense but sexy."

"Don't take it literally," he said, panting. "I'm not trying to fuck you. These are fantasies, not orders."

"I like your fantasies," she said, surprised by how much she did like it.

"Good, because if you keep doing that I'll keep talking."

"Keep talking," she said. "Please keep talking…"

She rubbed him harder now and he ground his hips up and into her hand. He seemed to really like the pulling maneuver so she did it again and was rewarded with a "Fuck" and "God, I want you to ride my cock."

She swirled her fingers around the tip and then tugged lightly on the whole shaft.

"If you're as wet as I am hard, you're drowning over there," he said.

She opened her fingers to knead him. Clover felt breathless and shaky and if she wasn't careful, she was about to start saying a few things herself.

"I want to fill all your holes up with my come."

Every dirty little thing he said kicked her body temperature up another degree and another. She couldn't remember being this turned on in her life. Nobody had ever said this sort of stuff to her before. Instead of being shocked by it, she was aroused, incredibly aroused. She was wet, she did want him inside her and she did want him to come in her over and over again. She wished she could tell him that the way he told her everything he was feeling, but the words were trapped in her brain so she told him how much she wanted him with her touch.

His chest rose and fell rapidly. His head fell back on the pillow. He was the most erotic, sexy, sensual, dirty-mouthed man she'd ever known, and if she could just tell him that, everything would be better.

"Say something, Clover," he said, and she heard the plea in his voice. "I'm feeling alone over here."

"I..."

"Say something. Anything."

"I want you," she said.

"How? Where?"

"Inside me. Deep."

She saw the outline of his smile.

"Good," he said. "You should."

"I mean it, Erick," she said. She loved the sound of

his name on her lips. "That wasn't a fantasy. I'm asking you to do it."

"Asking me to what? Say it. I don't want to do anything you don't want me to do."

"I want you inside me. Please."

"Tongue, fingers, cock?"

"All of them. But cock first."

"Now?"

"Please—"

He moved so fast she was on her back before she could say "and thank you."

She lifted her hips to help him slide her panties off. This was insane. They'd only had their first kiss three hours ago. But she felt like a runaway train, no stopping her or him or them or this. And she didn't want it to stop. Not now. Not ever.

Erick pushed her thighs apart with his knees and took his cock in his hand.

"Are you wet enough?" he asked.

"Drowning."

He braced himself over her and she lay flat on the bed beneath him, ready and eager and waiting. She flinched in pleasure as the tip of his penis grazed her swollen clitoris.

"Wider," he said, and she lifted her knees and spread her thighs. He pushed the tip through her wet folds and entered her. As he lowered himself onto her, his cock went deeper inside her. She heard a moaning sound, low and dirty, and realized it was coming from her.

"You're so fucking wet," Erick rasped into her ear. "And burning up inside." He slid his arm under her to hold her hard against his chest. She felt weak in his arms, weak and faint and small. She liked it. He pumped his hips into hers, pushing his cock deeper. Gasping she dug her fingernails into his shoulders as she pushed back against him. She didn't want him inside her. She *needed* him inside her. It was life or death. At least, it felt like it in the moment.

"That's it," he said as he thrust into her again. "Show me how much you want it. Show it to me, beautiful."

She opened her legs wide, dug her heels into the bed and pushed up and up against him as he bore down on her, thrusting harder, pounding her like he'd warned her he would. It was hard sex, not rough but she definitely felt everything all the way into her stomach. With him on top of her and his arms around her, holding her so tightly she felt like a princess in a book, being taken and ravished and used by some sort of barbarian warrior.

And she loved it.

He had her pinned down, nailed to the bed. She couldn't escape, couldn't move anything but her arms and her hips. And the best part was she didn't want to escape, didn't want to move from him. She just wanted to lie here underneath him and let him fuck her for the rest of her life.

She tried to tell him but he had something to say instead.

"Your pussy's so tight it feels like you've never been fucked before."

"I haven't."

Erick froze midthrust and looked down at her.

"Don't stop," she said, wrapping her legs around his thighs to hold him inside her. "Please, please, please don't stop."

"Not stopping," he said. "Not ever."

He kissed her mouth and she couldn't help but sigh with relief when he started to move inside her again. At first he was careful with her, too careful, like he was afraid to hurt her. She didn't want that. She wanted it like it was before. She lifted her hips again into his, letting him know with her body how much she wanted what he had to give her. He took the hint and thrust a little harder, then a little harder than that. She had to say something. If she were him, she'd be silently freaking out, so she had to tell him something to make him relax and enjoy it again as much as he had before.

"I wanted it to be just like this," she said.

"Like how?" he asked.

"Everything you do feels so good to me."

"Does this feel good?" he asked as he slowly pulled his cock out to the tip and thrust it back in.

"Yes… Again…"

He pulled back out to the tip, thrust in again, back out, in again, pausing before each thrust, making her wait for it, making her miss it inside her before giving it back to her.

"I want you to come for me," he said. "I want to feel it on my cock. Can you come? Are you close?"

Her thighs were tight as knots and her lungs burned and every time he entered her, her vagina clenched down onto him.

"So close," she said, nodding against his shoulder.

"Good. Come for me, then, baby. I need you to come for me."

He needed her to come for him… It should have intimidated her, but it didn't. He wanted her to orgasm as much as she did.

Erick released his rough hold on her to give her more room to move underneath him. She clutched the sheets in her fingers as he braced himself over her, his hands on either side of her shoulders. Where their bodies met and joined, she felt the most deliciously intense pulsing sensation, a rhythmic throbbing that she wanted to feel forever. He drove into her with long thrusts designed to draw every bit of pleasure out of the movement as possible. Each penetration grazed her clitoris and each withdrawal left her aching for the next thrust. It was happening; she was there, so close. Yes, this is how she wanted it to happen, how she'd always wanted it. It felt so natural, so right, so sexual and sensual and erotic. She didn't feel nervous anymore. She didn't feel scared. She felt filled up and open and wet. It burned but it didn't hurt. She couldn't get enough of Erick, enough of his cock. Writhing beneath him, Clover felt the most incredible tightening, like someone had wrapped a rope around her hips and pulled it taut and tight and tauter until it was ready to snap.

She heard Erick's breathing, heard him say her name, heard him say "fuck" a few times. She'd never found that word very sexy until it came from his mouth while he was in her body with nothing between them but his own T-shirt he'd given her to wear. She would keep this shirt until she died. He could have it back over her dead body and not a second sooner.

It was everything she'd always wanted it to be. The bed rocked beneath them and Erick put his entire body into fucking her so that she felt his every breath and his every thrust. The headboard rattled against the wall and she moved under him and with him, taking every inch of his cock into her. She was so wet it didn't even hurt, not one bit. Thirty years of pent-up need and desire and dreaming of being taken like this peaked in one perfect moment. With her eyes closed and her head back and her hips hovering inches off the mattress, she came hard, her inner muscles contracting in sharp spasms that left her panting and dizzy.

Erick's fingers were in her hair and he tilted her head back even farther. He kissed her throat, thrust in hard and came inside her. She could tell he was coming because he went silent, completely silent for the first time since penetrating her.

He lay on top of her and breathed into her ear while she sleepily kissed his naked shoulders, his neck, his chest. Good thing the lights were off so he couldn't see what she knew was a stupid-looking grin on her face. She felt drunk, tired, happy and sore, and she loved all of it.

Erick slowly pulled out of her and rolled onto his back. He took a heavy breath.

"Well…" he said.

"Well?"

He rolled onto his side and draped his arm over her stomach.

"That was unexpected."

"Imagine how I feel," she said.

"I am. Can I ask you one question?"

"Go ahead," she said. She'd expected more than one question. One question only was getting off easy.

"Why the hell were you still a virgin at thirty? And why didn't you tell me before I pounded you into the bed?"

"That's two questions."

"One's a follow-up to the first one. Two-parter."

"Can I ask you a question first?" she asked.

"Ask."

"Are you mad at me?"

5

ERICK COULDN'T BELIEVE his ears. Mad at her? Mad at her? Why the hell would he be mad at her?

"In what universe would a man be mad at the woman he'd just had incredible sex with?" he asked. "Tell me what universe so I know never to go there."

"So you aren't mad?"

"Of course I'm not mad. Surprised? Yes. Not mad."

Clover sighed, her relief palpable.

"Good. I probably should have told you but I got caught up in the moment. It was a good moment."

"Yeah, it was, wasn't it?" He touched her face, traced her smile. He was glad to see that smile. He'd never been with a virgin before and, as he was thirty-eight years old, he really hadn't expected this situation to come up. He didn't quite know how to feel about it other than happy he'd left her smiling. "So...any reason you want to share with me why you've never had sex before tonight?"

"It wasn't for lack of trying, I promise. And I've had some sex. Just not the big one."

"I can't imagine why someone as pretty as you, as

smart as you, as together as you, never…unless you didn't want to."

"I wanted to. It's kind of embarrassing."

"Clover," he said, shaking his head and laughing softly. "I'm naked. My semen is inside you. And you just had sex for the first time in your life—with me. I think it's safe to say we are way past being embarrassed with each other right now?"

"I had no idea there would be so much of it." She glanced under the sheet as if inspecting her wet thighs. "Like…a pint."

"That's been building up awhile. Stay there. I'll get a towel."

He left her in the bed and went into the bathroom. She had a stack of pretty white washcloths on the towel rack. Probably too nice to use for postcoital cleanup but that's what washing machines were invented for. He soaked the cloth in warm water, rung it out and brought it back to the bed. He switched on the lamp and found Clover looking sleepy, blissful, adorably rumpled and thoroughly, thoroughly fucked.

"I can do it," she said.

"You can do it but I want to do it," he said. "We're getting to know each other. Let me see you."

He pulled the covers down her body and he could sense her tensing. Gently he pushed her knees apart and even more gently he wiped his semen off her and out of her.

"No blood," he said. "That's good. I was a little rough there. Sorry."

"I liked it."

"You liked it rough?"

"I liked it with you," she said.

"And I liked it with you. I very much like this." He

opened her up with his fingers a little wider and looked at her open body. "You're beautiful here. But you're beautiful everywhere."

"Not exactly," she said. He tossed the washcloth into her clothes hamper and looked down at her again as she pulled the sheets up to cover herself.

"What do you mean 'not exactly'?"

"I mean…well…see?"

She lifted her T-shirt up and showed him her breasts. He whistled in appreciation to make her laugh. She didn't laugh.

"Don't take this the wrong way, but you have nice breasts, Clover. I don't know why you think I wouldn't agree."

"You can't see the scars?" she asked.

"Yeah, I can see them."

On both breasts she had scars, pale white and thin, running from her nipples to the bottom of her breasts and from there in a straight line to her armpits.

"They don't look weird to you?" she asked, wincing a little. "They look weird to me."

"They just look like breasts to me. Very pretty breasts with very light scarring. You feel comfortable telling me what happened?"

She pulled her—his—T-shirt down again, which he wished she wouldn't do but maybe it wasn't the best time for ogling her.

"I had breast reduction surgery when I was twenty-five. I used a little of my grandparents' money on that. The rest went into the business."

"Are you glad you had it done?"

"Definitely. I had back and shoulder pain and I couldn't find clothes to fit me right. I went from an E cup size to a small C."

"I didn't even know they came in size E."

"Special order only. Getting the surgery was a miracle. It was like someone gave me my life back. And my back back."

"I'm glad you feel better now. You look great."

"The scars are a lot lighter now. They used to be more gnarly."

"Scars are scars," he said. "They're just skin that's a different color."

"Thank you, Erick," she said with a sweet, shy and sleepy smile. If she kept looking at him like that, they were both going to be in trouble. "It's sweet of you to say."

"It's true," he said. It was. He didn't care about scars. He had a few dozen of them himself from nails, weed whackers and rotator cuff surgery. "Were you self-conscious about your breasts?"

"In high school...oh, it was awful," she said, shaking her head. "I've always been kind of shy but then it was like overnight I had these two huge beacons on my chest. And high school guys act like a girl with large breasts must be easy. Especially if she's a blonde. I hated the way they looked at me and talked about me. I started covering up as much as I could, hiding in my clothes, hiding from them."

"I feel bad about teasing you over your schooner nightgown now."

"No, it's fine. I like the way you tease me. I don't know why but when you tease me I feel better. It helped. I'm feeling more comfortable now. Much more."

"Good. I want to help. Sorry about high school. I might have been one of those hormonal dipshits who couldn't keep his eyes off you, too. Guessing college wasn't much better?"

"I went on dates but I had trouble trusting guys. Especially when they try to get your top off on the first date and call you a cocktease when you say no."

"Oops." He winced.

"You didn't try to get my top off on the first date. You got my bottom off on the first date."

"Whew. In all fairness to me—and we must be fair to me—getting your bottom off was your idea."

"True," she said, laughing softly.

"When I was twenty-five I got the money from my grandparents and decided to have the surgery. I had just started dating this really great guy—Tyler. Came from a pretty Christian family so he liked that I was still a virgin. But then I told him I was having the surgery and he freaked out. He said it was against God's will to change my body like that. I reminded him he'd had Lasik eye surgery. He said it wasn't the same thing."

"Something tells me Tyler wasn't a Christian. Something else tells me Tyler was a dick."

"You're right. He was a dick. I had the surgery, anyway, and he dumped me right after. Said I'd mutilated myself."

"Such a dick." Erick dropped his chin to his chest. "Men suck."

"You all really do suck. Really, really suck."

"Keep it coming. I'll go flog myself in the street in penance later. I want to hear it all."

"There's not much more. I started the nursery and got too busy to date. That was my twenties—back pain, humiliation, and very short, very crappy relationships. The nursery made me happy and dating made me miserable so I put all my attention on one and let the other kind of fall by the wayside. Meanwhile my older brother and his wife started having kids and my younger sister got married and started having kids. And I finally found someone I really liked abou three years ago and then I told him I'd never had sex before and…well…that was that. But we did fool around a lot. I'm not completely inexperienced. And I hate the word *virgin*. I'm a grown woman with sexual experience. Just not a lot of it."

"You do give very good hand jobs. Excellent. I give it five fingers out of five."

"I tried."

"You succeeded. I guess considering your history I can't blame you for not telling me you'd never had sex before. Men can get squirrelly about that stuff."

"You don't seem squirrelly."

"I might have been if you'd told me before. It wouldn't have stopped me from fucking you. I might have just waited a few days and gone a lot slower."

"Then I'm glad I didn't tell you. Ruthie calls it my 'little problem.' That's why she was joking about hiring me a male escort. At least I think she was joking about Sven."

"Oh, Sven."

"Good ole Sven."

"So my seventeen-year-old daughter has been trying to get her thirty-year-old boss laid? And to think I thought all she did at the nursery was water plants and answer the phone."

"I promise, hiring me male escorts was not in the job description. That was all her idea."

"The only bad downside of us sleeping together is that I can't call my parenting book *Kids Are Such Cock Blocks* anymore. Damn. It was going to be a bestseller."

"Sorry."

"Are you?"

"Not at all," she said. "That was…amazing."

"I like that word. Amazing. It implies that you were, you know, amazed." He waggled his eyebrows at her to make her laugh.

"I was amazed. I was lying there and thinking, 'Wow. I didn't think this would be worth all the trouble.' And you know what? It was worth all the trouble."

"I hope there's no trouble. You did say you were on the pill, right?"

She nodded. "I take it every day. You don't have to worry about that."

"When I had the sex talk with you know who, I said condoms all the time, every time. I love being a hypocrite. Not the best part of being a parent but definitely in the top five."

"In all fairness to you—and we must be fair to you," she said.

"We must."

"I wasn't kidding about the latex allergy. I got hives in the hospital after surgery because the doctor was wearing latex gloves. Although maybe I mentioned that so you'd think I'd had sex. I didn't want to freak you out."

"Not freaked out," he said. "You? It was your first time, after all. Feeling okay about it?"

"I feel pretty good," she said. "Very good, really."

"Good enough to go another round?"

"Hmm... I'm a little sore inside but we can try."

Erick shrugged. "We'll wait until you're ready. We had sex once and it's already more than I've had all year."

"We can keep kissing, though," she said. "I'd like that."

"Can I ask you something personal?"

"Isn't that all you've been doing for the last four hours?"

"Good point," he said. "Although I did ask where you got your brushed copper towel rack in the downstairs bathroom, and I don't think that's personal, right?"

"What's your personal question?"

"Are you comfortable with me kissing your nipples? Or are they off-limits?"

"Not off-limits. If the scars don't bother you…"

He shook his head and slid under the covers again, on top of her.

"They don't…" He pulled her shirt up to her neck. "Bother me." He flicked his tongue over her right nipple. "One bit." He flicked his tongue over her left nipple.

"I like you," she said as he gently sucked her nipple into his mouth and kneaded it with his tongue. "I like you very much, Erick Fields."

With his arms around her he pulled them onto their sides. He kissed her nipples for a long time, as long as she'd let him, which was thankfully a long time. He enjoyed it, definitely. She had beautiful breasts, perfectly symmetrical, and from the way her nipples hardened in his mouth, the way she moaned as he sucked her, he knew she'd retained all her sensitivity. But he didn't kiss her breasts solely because he enjoyed it. He wanted her to get over her self-consciousness. First she'd hidden her body under her clothes because of the size of her breasts, then hid herself because of the surgical scars. He didn't want her to hide herself anymore, not from him. He wanted her to see herself as desirable and as beautiful as he saw her. Desirable and beautiful and smart and she ran her own business and she was amazing with his daughter… The list of everything wonderful about Clover went on and on. He better be very careful or he was going to end up falling in love with her.

"Erick?"

He kissed a freckle on the swell of her right breast.

"Yes?"

"Now my nipples are getting sore."

He sighed. Heavily.

"I'll stop. If I must."

"Just for a little while. My body's not used to all this attention."

He slid up the bed and they lay face-to-face on her pillow. He took her leg in his hand and laid it over his hip. He could have slid his cock right into her but he didn't. He just wanted to be as close to her as possible.

"It'll need to get used to it—fast," he said. "I think I'm already addicted to your body." He ran his hand down her naked back. Such soft skin…he couldn't get enough of her.

"So do you want to keep doing this?" she asked. Her eyes were searching his face, and he saw the old nervousness back in those pretty blues.

"Having sex with you?"

"That."

"Yes, yes and yes. I want to have all the sex with you."

"What constitutes 'all' the sex?" She narrowed her eyes at him.

"Well…there's all kinds of sex. Oral. Anal—don't worry, it's not a deal breaker with me. Vaginal, which we've had and I'd love to have again a few thousand times. But you know, there's sweet sex, gentle sex, rough sex, dirty sex, sex in different positions, sex in different places, like cars, hotels, swimming pools— not recommended."

"No pool sex?"

"I've tried it and it's like pushing a tennis ball inside a coin slot. The lack of lubrication does not work. Maybe in books and movies but not in the real world. But hey, if you want to try it, we'll try it. You bring the coin slot and I'll bring the tennis ball."

"Not a fantasy. I've thought about sex by the lake but it's late November now. This is not outdoor sex season."

"There's always next summer."

"Next summer? Planning ahead?" she asked.

"I'm a very busy man in the summers. If you want lakeside sex, you have to book in advance."

She laughed and nodded. "I'll check my calendar."

"Let's see…there's also couch sex and kitchen-table sex. These sexings are a little overrated unless it's a really big couch and the fabric is Scotchgarded. Shower sex can be very good if there's lube handy."

"What's your favorite kind of sex?"

"Before tonight I would have said 'doggy style in the bed of a pickup' sex. My marriage fell apart pretty fast but we had a good honeymoon, that's for sure. But that was before tonight."

She raised her eyebrow at him.

"And after tonight?"

"After tonight I would say my favorite kind of sex is what you and I had. Surprise sex. Good-surprise sex. Didn't think I'd have sex with anybody today. And then I did and it was with you, who I've been trying not to like for a whole year. And not only that, you've never had sex before me and finding out I'm your first makes me feel really…well, it was a good surprise, let's just call it that. That's my new favorite kind of sex. Good-surprise sex."

"Weird," she said as she rested her head on his chest.

"Why's that weird?"

"That's my favorite kind of sex, too."

6

CLOVER WOKE UP alone in her bed. Nothing unusual there. She'd been waking up alone in her bed for thirty years.

But she also woke up naked in her bed, which was new. New and not at all unpleasant especially since she had no idea where her panties were, no idea where her T-shirt was and no care in the world to find them. She lay there for a while simply basking in the sense of victory she felt at finally having had sex last night. Mentally she patted herself on the back, shook her own hand and gave herself a high five. *Good job, Clo*, she told herself as visions from last night ran through her head. Erick was so sexy in bed. She'd always found him handsome but last night she learned the difference between attractive and sexy. The things he said to her…well, if he were here right now, they'd go for it again. But he wasn't here. Where was that man, anyway?

As she climbed out of bed she groaned a little, glad Erick wasn't here to see her wince. She was sore all over, inside and out. But such a good kind of sore. It wasn't painful, really. No, she was just aware of her body like she hadn't been aware of it before. Her nipples were a little swollen and her vagina felt tender and a little raw. She felt like a woman who'd had good hard sex last night and the best part of it was…she was and she had.

She took a long shower that did a lot to ease her full-body soreness, pulled on her bathrobe and brushed her teeth. When she reached for her ponytail holder and hairbrush she stopped and left her long hair down and damp around her shoulders. With a little makeup on, even she found herself kind of…sexy. A glance at the clock told her it was eight forty and that gave her a very good idea where to find Erick.

Sure enough, there he was on her deck, already at work replacing the rotted boards. She stood at the kitchen window with her coffee cup in hand watching him work. It was the first time she'd seen him doing what he did for a living. With Ruthie he was always laid-back, casual, easygoing as any man raising that smart-ass kid would have to be. But Erick at work was a different man than Erick at rest. His eyes were narrowed in concentration and everything he did was with precision and purpose. He looked good out there on her deck in his jeans and work boots with his hair slicked back from his forehead from the little bit of mist in the air. When he finished nailing down the last board, he stood up and jumped on the deck hard enough the dishes in the cabinets rattled. He moved a foot and jumped again. She smiled. He was testing her entire deck to make sure he hadn't missed a single rotted or loose board. Thorough. She liked that.

She poured a second cup of coffee, slipped her feet into her boots and walked out the back door to the deck.

"Morning, Mr. Fields," she said as she held out the cup.

"Morning, Ms. Greene. Hope I didn't wake you with all my banging," he said as he took the cup from her hand.

"I think I'd remember if I was woken up with a banging. Too bad I wasn't."

He grinned and leaned in to kiss her.

"I taste like coffee," she said.

"Why do you think I want to kiss you?" he asked.

"Oh, good point." She let him kiss her and it was so natural and comfortable she could almost forget for a second that last night had been her first time with this man or any man. With Erick it seemed like she'd done this all her life. A good feeling. The opposite of awkward.

"How's the deck?" she asked.

"Hanging in there," he said. "Eager to get you back in bed."

"My deck wants to get me in bed?"

"Oh…you said 'deck.'"

She grabbed him by the front of his shirt and kissed him again.

"You," she said, narrowing her eyes at him. "You make me happy."

"And you…make me coffee. And if that's not another word for happy we need to change the thesaurus." He pulled her even closer and she was grateful for the sudden influx of male body warmth. It couldn't have been more than fifty out this morning, which was great jeans-and-sweater weather and terrible "nothing but a bathrobe and boots" weather.

"So…" she said. "How is the dick this morning?"

"Needs a good rub down with sandpaper and a fresh coat of wax."

"That sounds painful."

"Oh…you didn't say 'deck,' did you?"

"You're ri-deck-ulous," she said. Erick groaned and buried his head against her shoulder.

"I fucked a woman last night who makes puns." He sighed. "What was I thinking?"

"Hmm…if you were thinking what I was thinking, you weren't thinking."

He lifted his head and her heart caught in her chest at the sight of his grin.

"Oh, yeah…that is what I wasn't thinking."

"I'm going to go in and make a little breakfast. Can you stay and eat or do you have to get to another job?"

"I'm due in Welches at ten but I can probably eat something quick. Do you cook?"

"Not much, but I can do eggs and frozen waffles. And yes, I know to unfreeze them."

"Sounds perfect. I'll teach you how to fry buffalo bacon this week. We can have it at Thanksgiving."

Her head fell back and she exhaled a moan.

"I forgot. I am hosting Thanksgiving this week. Why do I let my family talk me into this stuff?"

"Because you're too nice for your own good. But don't worry. After a few days with me, you'll be as ornery as I am. Or better—as ornery as Ruthie."

"I would kill to have half her spirit and guts."

"You seduced me in three hours. You have more spirit than you realize."

"I seduced you?"

"Completely. And you're doing it again." He wrapped his arms around her and kissed her with a warm coffee kiss. She loved the taste of his tongue and the heat of his mouth. Part of her wished she'd been doing this sort of thing for years. A bigger part of her was glad that she'd waited until Erick to find out how much fun it was to make out in the morning because you just can't wait until dark.

"Breakfast," she said, pulling back from the kiss. "Ten minutes."

"Ten minutes," he said with a little salute. "I'll just be over here minding my deck."

"It's my deck," she reminded him as she walked back toward the house.

"This week it sure as hell is," he called after her.

Clover felt good. Good enough to whistle as she cracked eggs into a bowl, put waffles in her toaster, poured orange juice into glasses. If this was how good she felt after having sex once, how good would she feel after the second time? The third time? Surely there was some law of diminishing returns, otherwise after ten times with Erick she'd probably have to be restrained for her own safety until she came down off the sex high. But she was determined to enjoy it while it lasted. After all, who knew what would happen after Thanksgiving? She didn't even know what to tell PNW Garden Supply about their offer yet. Her life would seriously change if she said yes to it. She'd have a lot of money, yes. But she'd have to pay a lot of taxes on that money, too. She'd be able to quit working for a couple years, but the nursery closed down, anyway, from the end of November to the end of February. And those were the longest, dullest months of her year every year. If she couldn't work all year, she'd go out of her mind with boredom. Unless…unless she had something to distract her from her boredom. Like a real boyfriend. Not a fake one just for Thanksgiving. But a real relationship that would let her make up for a lot of lost time… That was tempting…very tempting…

Clover rolled her eyes at herself. One night with

Erick and she was already planning their entire life together. Not good. She needed to roll back her expectations. Erick had agreed to play boyfriend through Thanksgiving. On Friday after her family left they'd have a nice long talk about whether they wanted to keep doing this on a more permanent basis. And if he said no, she would be okay. She'd miss him probably. She'd already kind of gotten used to having him around. Still, he had a daughter and he had a business and he might not be looking for anything serious. These things happened. Not the end of the world.

But maybe he'd say yes to a real relationship. And maybe they'd start working their way down that long list of all the different kinds of sex she needed to have...

Clover had just put the scrambled eggs onto the plates when her phone buzzed on the kitchen counter. She glanced at the number—Dad. Oh, goody.

With a sigh she hit the button and put the phone to her ear.

"Hi, Daddy, what's up?" she asked, putting a smile into her voice.

"Just checking in on my girl. Your mother wanted to know what you want us to bring for dinner Thursday."

"Oh, the salad, the cranberry sauce, the mashed potatoes and gravy...desserts."

"So everything?"

"No, not everything. I can do the turkey."

"You?" Her father sounded skeptical. She didn't really blame him. "You're going to cook the turkey?"

Ruthie had said her father could work magic with a Big Green Egg. Might as well let him cook the turkey. It would impress the heck out of her parents.

"Yes, we'll handle the turkey."

"We?" her father repeated just as Erick slid the

glass deck door open and stepped inside the house. She looked at him and mouthed, "Help," at him.

"Who is it?" Erick whispered.

Clover muted the phone quickly.

"Dad. I accidentally said 'we' would cook the turkey."

"We can cook the turkey," he said.

"What do I tell Dad?"

"Let me talk to him," Erick said.

"What?"

"Just let me talk to him."

"Okay, if you insist." Clover unmuted the call. "Dad?"

"Where'd you go?" her father asked.

"Sorry. The phone cut out for a second. You know I live in the middle of nowhere. Here. Erick wants to talk to you."

"Who is Erick?"

Erick took the phone from her hand and put it to his ear.

"Mr. Greene?" he said, and Clover tensed into a tight vibrating bundle of nerves. "Yeah, this is Erick, Clover's boyfriend. I hear I get to meet you all on Thursday."

Erick paused and winked at her.

"Nice to talk to you, too, sir," Erick said. "No, Clover was kidding. We can handle all the food unless you or your wife have something special you want to bring… The turkey? Yeah, we're cooking the turkey, too. What do you think? Fifteen-pounder enough for everyone?"

Erick tucked the phone against his shoulder and with his free hands he reached for her bathrobe cord. She swatted his hands away but that didn't deter him from putting his hands on her waist and pulling her to him.

Clover leaned against him, her arms around his back, and listened to her father chattering at Erick.

"Well, we got seven kids coming but only three of them are old enough to put much of a dent in the turkey. Fifteen should be plenty unless you all want to eat leftovers for a week," her father said.

"I better make some extra," Erick said. "My daughter will kill me if I don't. She's a vegetarian all year except between Thanksgiving and New Year's."

"You have a girl, too?"

"Yes, sir. Seventeen. Almost eighteen. God, I'm getting old."

"We get to meet her, too, this week?"

"She's with her mom and her stepdad in LA all week."

"Sorry to hear that."

"Swing by Clover's nursery next week and you'll meet her. She works for your daughter."

"That how you two met?"

"That's how we met. My daughter fixed us up."

"Good for her. Clover's a good one. Can you put her back on the phone?" Erick passed back the phone. He looked adorably smug. Already working his charm on her parents.

"Hey, Daddy," she said. "You and Erick work out the turkey?"

"We did. I like this Erick fellow," he said. "Even if he is at your house awful early…"

"I'm thirty years old," she reminded him.

"You might as well be twelve. Until you're married with kids of your own, you'll be my little girl."

"Well, I'm not married and I don't have kids of my own, and I'm still thirty. I have the birth certificate to prove it."

"You'll understand how it feels when you have your own babies. The sooner, the better."

"Right, the sooner, the better."

"Tell Erick you're not getting any younger."

"Dad, we just started dating. And two seconds ago I was your little girl. Now I'm getting old?"

"You know what I mean, sweetheart."

Clover sighed as quietly as she could. "Yes, Dad. I know what you mean. I'll see you all on Thursday."

"We're really looking forward to it," he said.

"You and me both. But can you do me a favor?" she asked. "Don't tell Mom and Kelly or anybody about Erick. I've got a lot to do this week and I don't want to be on the phone with them for hours on end."

"Your secret is safe with me," he said.

"Thanks, Daddy. Love you. Bye."

They hung up and Clover sighed again.

"What?" Erick asked as she rested her head on his chest.

"I'm supposed to tell you I'm not getting any younger so you need to hurry up and get me pregnant since I won't be treated like an adult until I have children. But I'm not supposed to be sleeping with you, either."

"So I'm supposed to knock you up, but I'm also supposed to do this without having sex with you?"

"Yes."

"This is going to be difficult. Or not. Got a turkey baster?"

"Welcome to the world of being a woman. We're not supposed to have sex, but we're also supposed to have kids. And we wonder why so many women are on Xanax."

"I'd be swallowing that stuff with a bourbon chaser if I were a woman. Damn."

"It's about to get worse," she said. "Dad can't keep a secret to save his life."

"How much worse?"

Clover's phone started to buzz again. All at once she was receiving a phone call and text messages from both Kelly and her mother with another text message coming in five seconds later from her sister-in-law.

"It's kind of insulting, isn't it?" she asked, holding up her phone. The first text message read, Boyfriend??? Oh, my God, it's about damn time. Finally! I'm so happy! Tell me everything. I can't believe we get to meet a boyfriend.

Clover shook her head. "It's the 'a' there that really hurts. We get to meet 'a' boyfriend, not 'your' boyfriend. As if it's such a huge shock I'd have a boyfriend at all. Thanks, sis. Just the self-esteem boost I needed."

Erick grimaced as he read the text.

"Pass the Xanax."

"And the bourbon," she said as Erick pulled her into his arms. "And to think, I was so happy this morning. Now I have to spend the rest of the day trying to calm down my entire family before they start planning our wedding for us."

"Or."

"Or?"

Erick took the phone out of her hand.

"I will teach you one of Ruthie's secrets for keeping her parents out of her life. It's a very simple secret and you will benefit from it greatly."

"What are you doing with my phone?"

"I am…" Erick pushed the button on the top. "Turning it off. Now no one can call you or text you. Or they can but you can't see the messages until you turn the phone back on again in say…twenty-four hours?"

"That's brilliant. Why did I never think of that?"

"Because you are a kind and thoughtful daughter who would never ignore your parents' phone calls. Unlike Ruthie, who once threw her phone into the Zigzag River after her mother called her one too many times that week."

"You know, the Zigzag isn't that far from here. You'll pass right over it on the way to Welches, won't you?" Clover entertained a brief and lovely vision of Erick throwing her phone out of his truck window and into the white-capped river as he drove over the bridge.

"Lost Lake is closer. But I don't think you need to do something that drastic. You just need to put this phone up here…" He put the phone on top of her kitchen cabinet where she wouldn't be able to reach it without a stepladder. "Out of sight, out of mind. No Xanax necessary."

"I feel better already. Want some breakfast?"

"I do want to eat. Definitely."

"You sit. I'll get the waffles out of the toaster."

"Oh, I didn't mean I wanted to eat breakfast," he said.

"Then what—"

Erick wrapped an arm around her waist and lifted her off her feet.

"Erick…" she said. "What the hell are you—"

"Kitchen-table sex," he said. "You need it."

"I need it?"

"Well…don't you?" he asked. "I would if I were you. Correct me if I'm wrong, but after that phone call and that text message, I'm pretty sure you need your pussy eaten."

He set her on the edge of the kitchen table and stood between her knees. His hands stroked her thighs and her hips and his mouth massaged her neck.

"Am I wrong?" he asked. "I've been wrong before."

Clover liked this table. It was solid oak and came with two leaves that turned it into a table that could seat eight to ten people. The kids would have their own table, but on Thanksgiving Day all the adults in the family would assemble around this table. This very table Erick had set her on. And he wanted to do that to her on this table? The Thanksgiving table?

Clover grinned.

"No," she said. "You aren't wrong."

"Didn't think so."

Erick kissed her on the mouth as he untied her bathrobe cord and pushed the robe off her shoulders. She inhaled sharply as the cool air touched her bare skin. Once more she was aware of her body. As Erick gently caressed her back with his rough fingertips, goose bumps popped up all over her and she shivered the most delicious shivers in his arms. He hadn't touched her breasts yet and her nipples were already hard. She felt so wicked and wanton leaning back on her hands as Erick kissed her naked neck, her naked shoulders, her naked breasts and stomach and thighs.

"Anyone ever do this to you before?" he asked as he gently put her flat on her back.

"Oral sex? Yes," she said. "But I was young and too nervous to come. Or maybe I could have and he just quit too soon."

"I'm not going to quit on you until you tell me to stop. Please...do not tell me to stop." Erick pressed a long deep kiss into the center of her stomach.

"I won't," she said. "I want it."

"My three favorite words to hear from a woman," he said while pushing her thighs open. He sat in a chair and pulled her hips closer to the edge of the table. "Tell me what feels good and what doesn't. Can you do that for me?"

"I can do that," she said. "For you."

"Good." Using his fingers Erick opened her labia wide. "So fucking good…"

She flinched a little as he flicked his tongue over her clitoris. It was such a sudden shock of sensation. He seemed to sense it was too much all at once. He licked her instead the next time, a long slow motion that made her fingers bunch up into fists. His mouth was hot on her and she could feel his warm breath on her most intimate parts, relaxing her, making her hot, making her writhe all at once. She sensed his tongue moving in a sort of spiraling motion, making circles around her clitoris and then dipping inside her. He had her thighs in his large strong hands and she opened her legs wider for him because it felt so good to do it. She realized as she did it that she wanted him to see her, all of her. She couldn't recall a time she wanted to be looked at by a man. Self-consciousness had kept her closed off and bundled up for her entire adult life. How freeing it felt to simply be naked and unafraid, naked and unashamed.

"You make me feel so good," she said, and she heard and felt Erick's soft laugh.

"That's what I like to hear when my head's between your thighs."

She smiled up at the ceiling as he kissed her clitoris again. She knew he thought she just meant he made her body feel good. But that wasn't all. He made her feel wanted, sexy, adored.

A wave of tenderness washed over her and Clover reached between her legs and put her hand on the back of Erick's head. His hair was soft and streaked with a few strands of gray. A grown man with life experience.

A mature adult man. Scars didn't bother him. Her lack of experience didn't bother him. All he cared about was her and her pleasure. Now she knew what she'd been doing wrong in her dating life before Erick. It wasn't that she'd been dating the wrong men. She hadn't dated any men at all, only boys. She liked having a real man in her life.

He seemed to sense her need to touch him, to connect. He took her hand and twined their fingers together and rested their joined hands on her bare stomach. Clover relaxed again against the kitchen table and let the pleasure of his mouth on her flow over her and into her and through her. The intensely pleasurable tension built quickly. Clover moved her hips in small pulses against and into Erick's mouth. He made a sound of approval as if her movements aroused him as much as they aroused her. He released her hand and grabbed her by both thighs, pushing them wider, pushing his tongue deeper into her. Clover found the edge of the table with her fingers and gripped it hard. Inside her stomach and hips, muscles twitched and flinched and tightened. She inhaled and couldn't exhale. Her head spun and her lungs burned. At last it hit her, her climax, deep inside her. She exhaled, arching on the table, stars dancing in front of her eyes. Somewhere far away she heard Erick chuckling and she knew he was laughing at the intensity of her orgasm. Let him laugh. She'd laugh, too, when she had the energy for it.

Slowly Clover lifted her head off the table and saw Erick wipe his mouth on the back of his hand. He smiled at her and it was the sexiest smile she'd ever seen on any man's face, and the best part was, she'd caused it.

"Thank you," she said.

"You're welcome. Mind if I…?"

"I want you to," she said. She laid back flat on the table as Erick opened his pants and slid the tip of his cock up and down the wet, throbbing seam of her body.

"Fuck, that feels good…" Erick said, his eyes closed as he slowly pushed into her. "Are you sore?"

"Only a little."

"I can be quick."

"Don't rush on my account."

"I might on my account, though." He took her breasts into his hands and lightly massaged them. She was too spent to do much more than lie there as he thrust into her, but she could watch. Had she ever seen anything this erotic? Erick with his lips parted and his eyes half-closed and his hands cupping and squeezing her breasts as his hips hammered into her. The table creaked under her and she was glad she'd shelled out the money for good solid oak.

Erick lowered his head and licked and bit her neck. He whispered things in her ear again, things like, "Fuck, your pussy feels so good wrapped around my cock," and various other wildly erotic musings. She wrapped her arms around his shoulders and let him pull her into a sitting position at the edge of the table. With his hands on her hips and her hands on his shoulders, he let go, fucking her with long deep strokes as she held her legs up and open for him. It was dirty. That's the only word she could think of to describe how it felt, how it must have looked. It was dirty and she loved it. He squeezed her hips hard and practically lifted her off the table when he came with a grunt. She dug her fingernails into the backs of his shoulders as he released inside her.

"That…" he said when he regained his breath. "Was…whew."

"You took the words right out of my mouth."

Erick laughed again and she loved that he laughed before sex, during sex and after sex. It made her feel so comfortable. He cupped her breast in his hand and kissed her on the mouth again. She tasted herself for the first time and was surprised by how sexy it was to know herself like that.

Slowly he pulled out of her and Clover clamped her legs shut tight while he grabbed a towel to clean them both off.

"Sex is messier than I realized," she said.

"My fault. Sorry."

"Don't apologize. I like it."

"You like it?" He sounded skeptical.

"Have you ever seen me wearing gardening gloves? Ever?" she asked.

"Now that you mention it…no."

"I like getting a little dirty," she said with a smile. "Makes you feel alive, close to nature. Real life isn't neat and tidy."

"Sorry, I didn't hear anything you said after the part about liking to get a little dirty. It put images in my head."

"I'm sure you'll tell me all about them eventually."

He laughed. "You know me already. I'd tell you all about them right now except I have to get to Welches."

She looked past him at the clock on the microwave.

"Oh, no, I made you late."

"It's okay," he said as he straightened his clothes and pulled on his jacket. "I'm a contractor, remember? Nobody expects me to be on time."

"Good point."

Clover slid off the table and tied her robe around her waist again, ran a hand through her hair. She had sex hair after all that. She'd never had sex hair before. So many firsts and all of them good. Maybe she'd survive Thanksgiving week, after all.

"I'll probably be working until six tonight. I'll swing by home and take a shower, be here around seven. We can eat in or go out and damn. What am I doing? You haven't even invited me back."

"Will you please come back this evening and stay the night again?"

"I don't know. I'm pretty busy."

She flicked the tip of his nose.

"Ow. I deserved that," he said.

"You did. So you'll be back around seven tonight and then we'll have dinner?"

"Yes, ma'am. If you change your mind or something comes up, text me. You have my number?"

"I don't." Clover put her hand on her forehead. "I slept with a man and I don't even have his phone number. Oh, my God, I have just done everything my mother told me never to do."

"It's fun, right?"

"So much fun."

"We skipped a few steps. No big deal. We're just overachievers. Tell me your number and I'll text you mine."

"You turned off my phone and threw it on top of the cabinet."

"Okay," he said. "Well, then, I guess I'll be back tonight and you can't change your mind."

"Not planning on it. But here's my number, anyway. If I know me, and I do, I'll get my phone back before you've made it to Welches."

She told him her number and he programmed it in his phone.

"I just sent you a text message that is nothing but the penis emoji."

"There's a penis emoji?"

"It's actually an eggplant but it's the best we have. Now we're caught up," he said. "I have your number and you have mine. We have plans for this evening. We are doing great at being a very healthy fake couple. You have a great day, and I'll see you tonight. Preferably naked."

He kissed her on the mouth and she was surprised by how quickly the kiss ended. It was a goodbye kiss, a simple one, and she liked it. Why did she like such a quick kiss? she wondered. Erick got into his truck and pulled out of her driveway. Because it made her feel like a real girlfriend, being kissed like that. That's how her parents kissed good-night when one was heading to bed before the other. It's how her brother, Hunter, kissed his wife goodbye before he left for work. It was a quick kiss because real couples could do that sort of thing and they could do that sort of thing because they knew they'd be together again soon and then they could kiss as long and as hard as they wanted.

Real couples kissed like that. But she and Erick weren't a real couple. He'd even called them a "fake couple." A "healthy fake couple" but still a fake couple. Yesterday she would have been fine with that. Yesterday she'd never had sex. Yesterday already felt like a million years ago.

This week just kept getting more and more complicated. Not only did she have to host her family for Thanksgiving and decide if she would sell her business, now she had a much more pressing engagement for this week—she had to figure out how to turn Erick from a fake boyfriend into a real boyfriend.

But not to make her parents happy and not to shut her siblings up, but for one reason and one reason only.

The man was so damn sexy.

7

ERICK PUT IT off all morning, all afternoon and almost all evening. He was back at his own house in his own bedroom and looking at a picture of his twenty-one-year-old self holding two-hour-old Ruthie in his arms at the hospital. What was he thinking having a child at twenty-one? Twenty-one was seventeen plus four which meant in four years if Ruthie followed in his footsteps, he could be a grandfather.

Horrible thought. He still felt like that kid in the picture holding that red-faced, squalling baby most days. Especially since Ruthie still looked like that when he got on her bad side. But he hadn't been lying to Clover. Ruthie really was the best thing that ever happened to him. And as much as that girl loved Clover, he had to do it. He had to bite the bullet, face the music and pay the piper all at once.

He had to call his daughter and tell her that he and Clover were sort of dating. No, not dating. They were "going out on a couple dates." That was better. Dating sounded serious. He didn't want Ruthie getting her hopes up that this was going somewhere. That would be bad, right? Getting her hopes up? Clover was amazing—

hardworking, smart, beautiful. So beautiful. Especially when she was naked and splayed out underneath him with her head thrown back in ecstasy and…

Wait. Maybe he wasn't worried about Ruthie getting her hopes up about them. Maybe he was worried about getting *his* hopes up about them. They'd only spent the one night together, but God, what a night. He still couldn't quite wrap his mind around being the first man to ever have sex with Clover. It didn't bother him—the opposite, really. He couldn't help but feel a little bit honored that she'd picked him for the job. He didn't know what he'd done to earn her trust and her body, but whatever it was, he wished she'd tell him so he could keep doing it.

Of course, he could hear Ruthie's voice in his head telling him he should never judge a woman's worth by her sexual history, that the concepts of sexual purity and virginity were outmoded views that reinforced a toxic patriarchy in America that sought to police women and their bodies. And while he agreed with her because he knew what was good for him—and also because she made a good point—he still couldn't quite wipe the stupid grin off his face every time he thought about being Clover's first. It had nothing to do with her and everything to do with him feeling like he'd been paid a very high compliment.

Not that he would tell Ruthie any of that. They were close when he wasn't threatening to lock her in her room for all eternity if she set another factory farm on fire, but he wasn't about to discuss his sex life with his daughter. Oh, hell, no. He knew his daughter too well. She might do something horrible like try talking about her own relationship with her on-again-off-again boyfriend, Ryo, who was back in Japan this semester, which meant Ruthie's phone bill was getting bigger than her paychecks. He should probably mention that to her when he called her. Daring to put a price tag on love would distract Ruthie from the news that he was dating Clover and might keep her from asking questions he didn't want to answer.

He called his ex-wife's house number and Ruthie picked up.

"Hello, this is the Technology Police. No one uses landlines anymore," Ruthie said in her usual dry deadpan voice. "Please hang up and call a cell phone like a normal person."

"This is your father speaking. You should know already I'm not a normal person."

"Pops, what is it? What do you want? I'm busy."

"Busy doing what?"

"Watching Evan play *World of Warcraft*," she said. Evan was her ten-year-old stepbrother, and while Ruthie had found it supremely disgusting when her mother had gotten pregnant eleven years ago, she'd apparently gotten over her disgust enough to actually enjoy spending time with her baby brother. Not that she'd admit to it. "He's so good at it and it's so fascinating to watch, please kill me."

"I sent you your phone today. You'll have it tomorrow."

"Okay, don't kill me. Just put me in a coma until tomorrow."

"It's your own fault for leaving your phone behind. And really unlike you."

"What can I say? I'm a girl and I was distracted by a cute puppy and some diamonds on the side of the road and whoops, airhead me."

"You set me up."

"Did it work?" she asked.

"It worked."

She cackled like a cartoon witch.

"I'm so evil," she said. "Did you ask Clover out finally?"

"Yes."

"Yes! I knew it! Goddess be praised. When are you going out?"

"Um, we had a date last night." Erick hadn't expected follow-up questions. He should have prepared some canned answer better.

"Already? Last night? Where'd you go?"

"Does it matter?"

"Of course it matters. Clover is easily my favorite person on the planet. You have to treat her well. Unlike me, she is classy."

"That she is. And yes, very unlike you."

"You didn't take her to the mac-and-cheese place, did you?"

"What's wrong with the mac-and-cheese place? They have truffle fries."

"Oh, Goddess, you did. Poor Clover. She deserves so much better than that. You could have taken her up to Timber Ridge. They're at least organic. I can't believe your first date with her was to a place with deer heads on the walls. What were you thinking?"

"Calm down. We didn't even go out to dinner."

"But you said you went out on a date last night."

"I did."

"You asked her out but you didn't go out? What do you mean you asked her out and you had a date but you didn't..."

Erick started sweating. When did it get so hot in the house?

"Ruthie, you're overthinking this—"

"You had a date with her last night and you didn't go out."

"We need to discuss your phone bill."

"Oh, my God."

Oh, fuck. When Ruthie said "God" instead of "Goddess," the shit was about to hit the fan.

"Calm down, Ruthless."

"You did it with Clover."

"I am your father and we are not discussing my private life."

Ruthie screamed.

Erick winced and held the phone away from his ear.

"Are you finished?" he asked when the sound died and the ringing in his ear subsided.

"I need a brown paper bag. I'm hyperventilating."

"Better than puking, I guess."

"How could you do that to Clover? She's a goddess. You are not worthy of her goddess-ness."

"That kind of hurts, kid."

"You know as well as I do she'd never done that before."

"This is not something I ever wanted to talk about with my daughter."

"And you know as well I do she didn't tell you that because she knew you'd wuss out on her."

"Apparently I am talking about this with my daughter."

"You know as well as I do that you didn't give her the first time she deserves."

"I have no comment here."

"Oh, Clover won't complain. No, Clover is a goddess and goddesses don't complain. She's too big for that. But on the inside, she's disappointed. Were there candles? Were you in a nice hotel room? Did you make it special? No. Of course you didn't because you didn't know. You just went right for it, didn't you?"

Erick screamed. It felt good. It felt right. He'd never screamed before like that. Felt primal.

"Pops?"

"Sorry, I was just trying to get you to shut the hell up. I hope it worked."

"It mostly worked. I'm calmer now."

"Good. Because I'm really done having this conversation with you."

"You and me both. I need to talk to Clover."

"You don't need to do that. She is fine. She is dandy. She is both fine and dandy and she does not need any relationship advice from a teenage girl."

"That's sexist and ageist, Pops. You're backsliding without me there to keep you in line. I should come back. Clover probably needs me."

"She is seeing your father, not you. She does not need you. She needs me."

"Hell, yeah, she does. She needs you to clean up the disaster you made of her first time."

"It wasn't a disaster. It was anything but a disaster."

"So you admit it. Ha! I knew it."

Erick rubbed the bridge of his nose and wondered briefly if he could legally put his seventeen-year-old daughter up for adoption.

"Now I know why ancient Greeks used to leave their kids to be raised by wolves. I think the wolves might have done a better job with you. Or eaten you," Erick said.

"They weren't the Greeks, they were Romans. And this is unfair. I did nothing wrong. You are the villain in this scenario. You had a responsibility here to do something awesome for someone awesome. Sexuality is a gift from Mother Nature and we honor it by honoring Her and we honor Her by honoring each other and the only sin in this world is to dishonor the gifts we're given by treating them lightly or taking them for granted."

"Are you a druid now? I can't keep up."

"Listen, I know Clover. She's too nice to complain, but inside, she probably wishes it had been a little more romantic, but she doesn't know how to ask for what she wants."

"Romantic? That doesn't sound very feminist."

"Please, Pops, I'm a third-wave feminist. We get what we want, and if we want romance, we get romance. And I know Clover. Under that boring turtleneck and fleece vest combo beats the heart of a true romantic. Now go and make things right. Don't call me again until she's the happiest woman on earth."

"Are you mad at me for dating your boss?"

"I don't care what you do with my boss. But I do care what you do with my friend. Clover is my friend. And I'm not mad, I promise."

"You aren't? You sound mad."

"I'm not mad at you. I'm just… I'm disappointed."

That hurt. That stung. He'd rather she be mad at him. Wait a second, he was the parent here. What was happening?

"I don't want to disappoint you. But this is really none of your—"

"None of my business, I know," Ruthie said. "Clover is an adult. But, Pops, she's been wounded. Crappy ex-boyfriends, family who makes her feel like shit. She keeps it all on the inside and lets it eat at her. You have to step up."

"Step up? What does that mean in any language I can understand?"

"It means Clover gave you a gift."

"Didn't you say virginity was a sexist outmoded concept created by men—"

"I'm not talking about virginity. I'm talking about trust. She trusted you. You have to honor the gift of her trust. Honor the gift, Pops. Honor. The. Gift."

"Honor the gift. Okay. I can do that."

"You can do that."

"Now that I'm honoring the gift, we need to discuss your phone bill," he said.

"I can't talk about that right now. I'm in too much shock. Call me back when you've done right by Clover. I love you, Pops. Even when I yell, even when I'm disappointed, I still love you and I always will."

With that she hung up and Erick stared at the phone in his hand for a very long time.

He was so glad they'd stopped at one kid. Teenage twerp thought she knew everything about everything. Clover was not disappointed about last night. She enjoyed it. She had an orgasm, a strong one. She was smiling ear to ear after and she fell asleep in his arms, still smiling. And she was smiling this morning when she brought him a cup of coffee out onto the deck. That was not the smile of a disappointed woman. Yeah, maybe it could have been more romantic, but that wasn't his fault, was it? He didn't know it was her first time. Then again, even if it hadn't been her first time, it was still their first time together. Maybe he should have brought flowers. Maybe he should have lit some candles. Maybe he should have honored the nature goddess, whoever that was.

Nature. Clover did like nature. Any woman named

Clover would have to like nature. And when they talked about favorite types of sex last night she said something about sex by the lake. Well, it was forty degrees out and raining so that probably couldn't happen.

Erick narrowed his eyes.

Or could it?

He checked his phone and saw that while the talk with Ruthie had drained his spirit, it hadn't drained the last of his battery. He scrolled through his phone looking for a number and then dialed it. It rang twice. A woman's voice answered.

"Hello, Lost Lake Village Rentals, Joey speaking."

"Hey, is Chris there? It's Erick Fields and—"

"I know who you are," she said. "You did the siding on our house."

"That's me," he said. "Hope you like it."

"Love it. It's gorgeous. You do fantastic work."

"Thank you. I needed to hear that." Glad one woman around here appreciated his handiwork. "Is Chris around?"

"In the shower, but if it's a billing issue, you can talk to me. I'm the property manager."

"Not a billing issue. His checks never bounce. I wanted to see about borrowing one of the cabins for a night. Not borrow, I can pay for it. I know you aren't open yet but I wanted to surprise my girlfriend."

"You can absolutely borrow one of the cabins for the night," Joey said. "And no cost. We don't have towels or anything in the houses yet, but most of them are furnished. And don't pay us. Chris said you gave him a huge discount on the siding. You just have to promise to leave us a good Yelp review."

"That I can do."

"What are you looking for?"

"You have anything that overlooks the lake?"

Joey laughed softly and it was a good laugh. The laugh of a happy woman having a good idea. He liked that laugh.

"I know just the place."

CLOVER SHOULD HAVE kept her phone off. Why did she bother turning it back on? Oh, yeah, Erick. Just in case Erick called her or texted her, she turned her phone back on. As soon as she did, she regretted it.

There they were. Ten text messages—four from her mother, three from her sister, one from her brother and two from her sister-in-law. Three voice mail messages—one from her mother, one from her sister, one from her father. And then there were the emails. One from everybody—father, mother, sister, brother. And all of them wanted to know, "Who's Erick? How'd you meet him? What's he like?"

She didn't want to keep ignoring her family mainly because they wouldn't shut up until she answered their questions. But if Clover called her mother and told her about Erick, then her mother would tell everyone in the entire family and maybe she would be spared the telephone tsunami.

With a heavy sigh and absolutely no desire to have this conversation whatsoever, Clover sat at her big oak table, the very same one she and Erick had sex on that morning, and called her mother.

"Where have you been?" were her mother's first words. Not "Hello." Not "Hi." Not "There's my daughter!" This was already a terrible idea.

"Working, Mom. Just working."

"I thought the nursery was closed for the winter."

"It is, but I still have to work. There's billing and payroll. Plus I got an offer—"

"Your father said you're seeing someone. Is this true?"

Okay, so maybe Clover wouldn't tell her mother about the buyout offer.

"I am."

"Well…tell me everything."

"There's not much to tell. I'm seeing someone. His name is Erick. With a *K*. Also a *C*. A *C* and a *K*."

"How'd you meet him?"

"Through work."

"What's he do for a living?" her mother asked, which was code for "How much money does he make?"

"He's a carpenter. I think that's what he'd call himself. He does cedar decks and cedar siding. Basically anything with cedar. It has natural insect repelling properties and—"

"Your father tells me this Erick has a daughter. Is that true?"

"I don't know why Dad or Erick would lie about having a daughter."

"Clover, I'm only asking because it's important."

"How is Erick having or not having a daughter important?"

"You don't think it's important?" Her mother sounded horrified.

"It's important to him. No idea why it's important to you."

"If you're dating him, everything about him is important to me."

"Wait," Clover said. "Are you dating him? Or am I dating him?"

"You are my daughter."

"So we're both dating him?"

"Clover, I have no idea what's gotten into you, but I'm not thrilled with this attitude. Why won't you answer my questions? Is this your new boyfriend's doing?"

"Yes, my kind, funny, handsome, hardworking, thirty-eight-year-old boyfriend is forcing me against my will to not answer your personal questions."

"I do hope you're joking."

Clover sighed. Heavily. So, so heavily.

"Yes, Mom. I'm joking. Erick isn't here. He's at work. We met at the nursery. We like each other. Nothing is serious yet. You'll meet him on Thanksgiving. That's all you could possibly need to know about him and me and us. Isn't it?" Clover decided to put her mother on the defensive. Better to ask questions than be interrogated.

"I don't know about that. Your father said Erick was at your house at eight thirty this morning."

"He was fixing my deck. He does that sort of thing. It's what he does for a living."

"He didn't charge you for fixing your deck, did he? That's not very—"

"Oh, my God, no. He didn't charge me. He's a good guy. You should be happy I'm seeing him."

"Of course we're happy you're dating anyone, dear."

Clover didn't reply to that. Perhaps if she clammed up and said nothing her mother would get the hint. And a comment like that didn't deserve a reply. They'd be happy with her dating anyone? Anyone at all? A random dude off the internet? An ex-con with neck tattoos of AK-47s? A suspected serial killer? Anyone?

"It's very interesting that you don't want to talk about him. Your first boyfriend in a very, *very* long time and you don't want to discuss him?"

"He's not my first boyfriend in a very, *very* long time."

"You've dated other people without telling us?"

"It's not out of the realm of possibility. I am thirty years old. I do get to have a private life, don't I?"

"You act like I'm interrogating you."

"You are."

"All your father and I care about is your happiness."

"That's all you care about? Not Kelly or Hunter or your jobs or each other? Just my happiness?"

"You know perfectly well what I mean. The only reason I ask you these questions is because we care about you. We want you to be happy."

"I'm happy. Nothing else to see here."

"You still haven't told me about this girl of Erick's. How old is she?"

"She's seventeen. She's also my assistant at the nursery."

"Seventeen? That's awfully old."

"When did seventeen become old? What does that make you and me?"

"Seventeen is old when that's the age of your boyfriend's child. If he has a teenager, he might not want any other children. Have you thought about that?"

"Why on earth would I think about that?"

"You shouldn't be dating someone who doesn't want to have children."

"He has a daughter. Obviously he wants children, otherwise he'd have given full custody to his ex-wife. He didn't. He has full custody of Ruthie and he lets Ruthie visit her mom whenever she wants. Because he's a great dad."

"Clover, honey, you aren't understanding me. I'm sure he's a wonderful father to his girl. But if he has a teenager, he probably won't want to have a baby. He might not be a great choice to be the father of your children."

"Fine. Ruthie's fantastic. If she were my stepdaughter, I'd be thrilled. Although we are getting ahead of ourselves. He hasn't proposed yet. I haven't even been to his house yet."

"You don't mean that."

"I do mean it. He comes to my house."

"No, I mean, you don't mean that you'd be happy to be only a stepmother."

"Pretty sure I meant that. You don't know Ruthie. She's a pretty amazing kid. And by kid I mean fortyfive-year-old CEO trapped in the body of a teenage girl. She really could take over the nursery if I stepped down."

"She sounds wonderful. A delight. And we are all thrilled you're seeing someone, but—"

"Why?"

"What?"

"Why are you all thrilled I'm seeing someone? That's not something for you all to be thrilled about me. Me being thrilled makes sense. It's pretty normal behavior for an unmarried thirty-year-old grown woman to go out on dates."

"We're thrilled because we want you to be—"

"Happy. Yes. You want me to be happy."

And boy, was she happy right now. Happy happy happy. So freaking out of her mind happy she could scream.

"Your happiness is so important to me and your father. But happiness is more than just enjoying yourself. You do have to think about the future. You have to consider things like whether the men you date will want to have children."

"The man I'm dating has a child. He wanted children. He had one."

"His child. Not your child. Clover, I am a mother and I understand things you don't. You will never love anyone on earth like you love your own babies. You need to think about these things when you're choosing a life partner. You can't just date anyone you like."

"A life partner? Did you miss that portion of the conversation where I said I've never been to Erick's house? We're not quite at life partner stage."

"He must not be that serious about you if he hasn't invited you over yet."

"Or maybe he's very serious about me and he just likes my house better."

"So he comes over to your house a lot?"

"Mom, I have to go. Erick's calling. We're figuring out dinner plans."

"I didn't hear your phone beep."

"I did," Clover said. "Gotta go. Love you, Mom."

"Clover, we're not done talking. You call me back as soon as you're off the phone with him."

"I have to get ready for dinner. I'll see you on Thursday."

"Clover—"

"Thursday, Mom."

"Clover Greene—"

"Yup, that's my name all right. Bye!"

8

CLOVER HUNG UP on her mother. She'd never done that before. She'd never hung up the phone on her own mother. If only she could say it felt good, but it didn't feel good. Quite honestly, she felt like shit. Thrilled? Her family was thrilled she was dating someone? That would make sense if she'd been in a car accident and the doctors said she wouldn't survive and, lo and behold, six months later she was walking, talking and dating again. That would be an accomplishment. That would be something to be thrilled about. And all that stuff about Erick and babies? Where did her mother get off saying she shouldn't date a man with a teenage daughter? Her mother knew nothing about Erick. Erick could want zero babies or twenty babies and her mother wouldn't know. Clover didn't even know if Erick wanted more children. Clover didn't know and Clover didn't care. All she cared about was surviving the holiday without losing her mind, and if this was how her family was going to act, she might as well check herself into the hospital and stay there until January 2.

She put her head down on the table and forced herself to breathe. She had to breathe. If she didn't breathe, she would cry, and she didn't want to cry. When her family got to her like this she'd cry and it would take an hour before she could make herself stop. In, she breathed. Out, she breathed. In…out… Erick was wonderful… she breathed that in. Erick liked her and respected her… she breathed that out. Her business was a success and she had a lot to be proud of…she breathed that in. She didn't need her family's approval to feel good about her life…she breathed that out.

Clover heard a sound, a soft tapping on glass. She raised her head and saw Erick standing on her deck, knocking on the back door. When she opened the door she didn't let him inside. She just stepped forward into his arms.

"Whoa, baby. What's wrong?" he asked, pulling her close to him, wrapping his arms tight around her.

"I called my mother. Why did I do that?"

"Temporary insanity?" he asked, and she laughed.

"That's definitely it."

"What did she say? Tell me all about it so I can tell you how wrong she is."

"Give me a minute. I just… I need this." As embarrassing as it was to stand on her deck in the drizzle and cling to Erick like a life preserver, she did it, anyway, because someone in need of a life preserver clung to it no matter how ridiculous she looked or felt doing it.

Erick held her against him. He ran his large strong hands up and down her back, massaged her tight shoulders and kissed the top of her head.

"Tell me all about it," he said softly. "Get it out."

"It's like…" Clover paused and tried to figure out a way to explain it. "It reminds of something that happened right before I had my reduction surgery. I was a little overweight—only about twenty pounds, but it was enough I couldn't fit into my favorite clothes. The older I got, the harder it was to deal with my breasts. I couldn't jog or even go for long walks. So I had the surgery and could finally exercise. Between the surgery in July and Christmas when I saw my family again, I'd had the reduction and lost the twenty pounds. I went down two dress sizes. That's it. Not a huge change, right?"

"Nope."

"But when my family saw me, they went crazy. They told me over and over and over again how great I looked. Compliments, right? I mean, a normal person would take compliments as compliments. But it didn't feel like a compliment. It felt like an insult. Was I *that* hideous before I lost the twenty pounds that they'd make that big a deal out of losing the weight? I thought I looked pretty good before, you know?" She looked up at Erick. "So now it's happening again. They're acting like it's some kind of miracle I'm dating someone. They're 'thrilled' for me. I didn't win the lottery. I didn't wake up from a coma. I'm seeing someone and they're thrilled. My mom says she's thrilled. My sister is freaking out. Even my brother and his wife texted me trying to get details about you. All thrilled, they say. And I should be thrilled they're thrilled, right? Am I the worst daughter ever?"

"No."

"Then what is it?"

"Well…you may not want to hear this, but I have a theory about your family."

"I want to hear your theory. What do you think it is?"

"To use a technical term, they're all a bunch of assholes."

Clover's eyes flew wide-open. She took a step back from him.

"What?"

"Your family sounds like they're assholes. No offense. I've got a few assholes in my family, too. Ruthie has more than once accused me of being one of them."

"My mother loves me, Erick. She wants what's best for me. She just doesn't know how to show it without making me feel…".

"What? How does your mother make you feel?"

"She makes me feel terrible about myself."

"And your father?"

"Kind of terrible."

"And your siblings?"

"They're not as bad. They only make me feel really crappy sometimes."

"Only sometimes? You know what they call someone who makes you feel terrible about yourself? They call that person an asshole. Say it. You'll feel better."

"I'm not going to call my family assholes. They love me."

Erick put his arm around her and steered her to the table. He pulled out her chair and she sat down. He sat down in the chair facing her.

"Your family does love you. And I'm sure they aren't actual assholes. They probably have no idea they're making you feel so bad. But that isn't an excuse. They shouldn't make you feel bad. They should do what normal healthy families do and ignore you and your personal life until you screw up and they have to bail you out of jail. I'm speaking from experience here."

"My family does not ignore me. I wish they ignored me. I'd kill for them to ignore me."

"We'll make it easy on them."

"How?"

"We're going to go away for two days. If you want

to. I'm not making you. Ruthie says men shouldn't dictate what happens on dates. I'm not dictating, only suggesting. I suggest we go away for two days."

"Away? Where away?"

"We're going to go all the way…five miles from here."

"I think they have phones five miles from here. Five miles from here isn't outer space. Unless we're going five miles straight up."

"Not straight up. Straight northwest. And it'll be like space because you aren't taking your phone with you. I talked to Chris Steffensen's girlfriend, Joey, who's also his property manager. She's letting us test out one of their new rental cabins for two nights. We're going to leave your phone here at this house. In case of emergency, we'll have my phone to call 911 if a bear tries to get in the cabin or something. And while your phone is here, we'll be there—eating, sleeping and having all the sex. What do you say to that?"

"Two days without answering my phone? My family will freak out."

"How will you know they're freaking if they can't reach you?"

"They'll freak out ten times as much when they do reach me."

"You won't see them until Thanksgiving. They're not going to freak out on Thanksgiving because I'll be there. Then they'll meet me, it'll calm them down when they see how great I am—"

"You are pretty great."

"I am and I'm even better at faking being great. I'll charm their pants off—not literally—and they'll finally shut up about your personal life because they will finally see with their own judgmental eyes that you are in these two very capable hands."

He held out his hands in front of her, palms up. They were quite capable-looking hands. They'd stripped her panties off her in a split second last night, massaged her breasts this morning and fixed her deck. Truly talented hands.

She put her hands in his, and he wrapped his fingers around hers, then lifted both her hands to his lips and kissed the backs of them.

"How does that sound?" he asked.

"It sounds pretty good," she said. "Especially the part about being in your hands."

"That was my favorite part, too." His dark eyes twinkled mischievously. "I think you'll like this place. I've already swung by and checked it out. It's nice."

"Do I need to bring anything?"

"I stocked the fridge already and brought over towels and stuff. They aren't quite ready for business but the furniture's all there, the appliances work and the electricity and water are running. Pack a bag for two nights and relax, because I've taken care of everything else."

She liked the sound of that. Someone else, someone who wasn't her, taking care of everything? When had that ever happened in her adult life?

"I'll go pack, then. I promise I'll leave the schooner sail here."

"Bring it if you want. It'll end up on the floor like anything else you put on."

"That sounds like a challenge."

"Does it?" he asked as he stood up and leaned back against the table.

"What if I'm wearing something so sexy you don't want to take it off me?"

"The lingerie has not been invented that is sexier than the naked female body—yours specifically. But if you want to play that game, I'm up for it."

"We'll see what I have hidden in my closet…"

She started up the stairs and Erick stopped her by saying her name. She stood on the bottom step and he came to face her.

"What is it?" she asked.

"Don't ask me why I'm asking this, but please tell me the truth. Are you disappointed with last night?"

She narrowed her eyes at him.

"What? No, of course not. Last night was…" She paused to search for a word. She couldn't find one good enough so she went with a classic. "Wow."

"It was wow?"

"Wow-wow," she said, blushing. "And a little whoa, too."

"Okay. Glad to hear it. I wouldn't want to have accidentally, you know, dishonored the gift of your trust in me."

"You told Ruthie."

He raised his hands in surrender.

"I didn't. I swear. She knew, anyway. I said you and I went out and that's all I said and then it was like she read my mind or something. I think she can do that."

Clover laughed. "It's okay. She's done that to me, too. I'll say one meaningless harmless thing like 'I feel like I haven't had a day off in a year' and two minutes later she'll have figured out that I haven't been on a date in forever and that I'm scared of dating because the last guy I went out with was such a jerk. She's told me many times I have to honor the gifts Mother Nature gave to me and that's the only way to overcome my feelings of failure."

"Do you actually understand any of what she's saying?"

"About half of it. But that half is pretty profound. She says I'm so contented and happy at work because Mother Nature made me one of Her handmaidens, and that by bringing plants into the world and tending them, I'm caring for Her children like a second mother. I am a midwife to Mother Nature. Sounds pretty impressive, right?"

"It really does. Much more impressive than what I am. She said if Mother Nature was the queen bee, I'm a drone, but I should be pleased with my role, however seemingly meaningless it is, in the cycle of life."

"That seems to imply your only reason for existing was to mate and have Ruthie."

"She would probably agree with that."

"I hope she wasn't too hard on you about, you know, you and me."

"She said I probably disappointed you because you're too nice to ask for what you want."

"I remember asking for what I wanted last night, and getting it. You remember that part?" she asked.

"I remember that part. My parts remember that part…" He put his hands on her waist. She had on jeans and a T-shirt, not a turtleneck, just a T-shirt, and it was nice to have her neck exposed so Erick could kiss it.

Which he did. Right there on the stairs he kissed her neck and her throat.

"I won't ever forget that part," she said, tilting her head to the side so he could kiss her under her ear in case he wanted to. Apparently he wanted to. "I didn't tell you because I wanted it to happen naturally without a lot of second-guessing and I didn't want you to worry about me and I really didn't want me to worry about you worrying about me. That's what I wanted. That's what I got. I didn't think it would happen so soon, but I also didn't realize how incredibly sexy you were until I got you into bed. So no, you didn't disappoint me. The opposite, in fact."

"Good," he said, pausing to nip her neck with his teeth. "That's what I needed to hear. But…"

"But?" She pulled back to meet his eyes.

"I do think Ruthie might be right and you may have a little bit of trouble asking for what you want. That you haven't asked your family to back the hell off and leave you alone is a good sign that maybe, just maybe, the kid is right about that."

Clover rocked her head from side to side, considered what he said and then nodded.

"She might be right about that."

"So…from now on, please be open with me. You're not going to hurt my feelings if you ask me to do something that I'm not doing or you tell me to stop doing something I am doing that you're not into. We're going to have a lot more fun together if we're both honest with each other, in and out of bed. Cool?"

"Cool."

"Is there anything you want to tell me before we leave? Anything you want us to do the next couple of days? Any other firsts we need to take care of?"

"Well… I've never given a blow job to completion. I feel like maybe that's something I should learn how to do. Do you think you could teach me?"

"No, that's not something I'm interested in."

She raised an eyebrow at him in suspicion.

"You're telling me you aren't into blow jobs?"

"Not my thing, no. Sorry."

"You're lying right now, aren't you?" she asked.

"Through my teeth." He nodded. "Now I know how Pinocchio felt."

"Your nose getting longer?"

"Something's getting longer. Now please go pack before we end up having staircase sex, which I had once and it was not good for anyone involved. Hurry. Go. Please."

She kissed him on the mouth because she could, because she wanted to, and she was thoroughly enjoying giving herself permission to do what she wanted to do.

"Going."

Erick slapped her ass when she turned around and a laugh of pure pleasure burst from her. Being in a relationship, even a fake one, with a man like Erick was seriously fun. She should have done this years ago. Then again, she didn't know Erick years ago and she couldn't have picked a better man to be her training boyfriend. He was definitely worth the wait, she decided as she opened up her closet and pulled out her suitcase. Into it she threw a couple pairs of her favorite jeans, warm wool socks, hiking boots, a couple favorite long-sleeved shirts and sweaters. She spied a pink-and-black bag in the corner of her closet, a pink-and-black bag that had been in that corner of her closet for several years. She took out the tissue paper and examined the contents. It should all still fit. And if Erick kept his promise, it wouldn't matter, anyway. Anything she put on tonight would end up on the floor in minutes.

She finished packing and went back downstairs. Erick had a bag in his hand and she saw he'd filled it with food from her cabinets and fridge.

"I don't know what you like to eat," he said. "I put some of your stuff in here so you'll have it."

"That's very thoughtful."

"You really eat pumpkin spice yogurt?"

"Who doesn't?"

"I'll tell you a few names once I'm done throwing up in my mouth."

"Oh, hush. It's good. Are you ready?"

"I am. Where's your phone?"

"In the bathroom upstairs."

"You promise?"

"I promise. I don't want that thing around any more than you do."

"Then let's go. Our palace awaits."

She locked the doors and turned off most of the lights and in minutes they were in Erick's truck heading to the rental, all of five miles from her own house. She did feel a little silly about spending two nights in a cabin that was so close to her own place. Like everyone else, she lived in the woods—sort of. There were trees everywhere, anyway. And she was within walking distance of the river. Could this little Lost Lake cabin be that much different from her own place? No big deal if it wasn't. She didn't care about the cabin. All that mattered to her was that Erick wanted to stay there and he wanted to stay there with her, just her, for two entire days. She would have stayed in a creepy motel with him if he'd asked. They could have creepy-motel sex, which was surely on the list of types of sex that could be had. Cabin sex sounded much better, but then again, as good as Erick looked right now in his khaki cargo pants and his long-sleeved navy T-shirt stretched tight over his broad chest, she wouldn't say no to creepy-motel sex right about now. Or any sex. At all. Anywhere. As long as it was with him.

"Here we are," he said. "Not bad, right?"

Clover didn't reply. She couldn't reply. Her jaw was on the ground and she hadn't picked it up yet.

Erick hopped out of his truck and walked to her door, opening it for her.

"I thought you said this was a cabin," she breathed.

"It is a cabin. A big fucking cabin and a big cabin for fucking. Nice, right?"

"Nice, yes. That's the word we'll use."

It wasn't nice. It was stunning. Perched at the edge of Lost Lake was a two-story mountain cabin with a glass chandelier inside hanging from the lofted ceiling. She knew that because Erick had left the light on so she could see it through the wall of windows. The entire east wall was nothing but glass. Although the sun had set, she could see that the cabin had been painted an elegant blue-gray and that a deck extended over the water. They walked side by side to the front door and as Erick pulled the key from his pocket Clover stepped out onto the deck. She set her bag down by the steps and walked to the railing.

She looked up and saw the outline of the clouds. The moon must be behind them, lighting them up from behind. If she squinted she could see the outline of the snowcapped peak of Mount Hood.

"It'll be incredible in the morning," Erick said. "That wall faces right into sunrise."

"It's incredible right now," she said. "I love the sound of wind on water. There's nothing quite like it. Always sounds like it's trying to tell you something. That sounds stupid. I don't know why I said that."

"It doesn't sound stupid," he said, standing behind her with each hand on either side of her so that she stood in the triangle of his arms and the deck railing.

"It sounds like something Mother Nature's handmaiden would say."

Smiling, she leaned back against his chest. The night air was cool but not cold, not at the moment. No need to rush inside quite yet. A perfect moment to simply be. The pine trees rustled as the wind shook them. Crows cawed and owls hooted. Maybe she was Mother Nature's handmaiden, and maybe Mother Nature was saying thank you for all the hard work she'd done over the years. Maybe Mother Nature had sent her Erick, too. Any man as good with wood as he was surely had been blessed by someone. She felt blessed in this perfect moment. Blessed because she was in it. Blessed because Erick was in the moment with her. Blessed because she knew it was perfect.

"I feel better already," she said. "Just being here makes me feel better."

"Nothing like a couple of days on the lake to clear your head."

"It's not the lake, although it's beautiful here. It's not nature. It's not the forest or the mountain. I feel better because I'm with you, and you did this for me."

She turned her back to the lake, to all the loveliness of it, and faced Erick. He was an even better view.

He dipped his head and kissed her on the mouth.

"Weird," he said against her lips.

"What is?"

"I feel better with you, too. It's almost like we like each other or something."

"Or something."

"You want to see inside the house?"

"I would love to."

He took her by the hand and led her to the door. She'd expected the room with the chandelier to be the living room. And maybe it could have been or should have been, but it wasn't. She walked down three steps into a sunken bedroom that held a king-size bed facing the lake. A bed right on the lake. If she broke the bottom window water would rush right into the room.

"Erick...this is..." Romantic. Breathtaking. Everything she could have wished for and more.

"You said you wanted to have lake sex. Not easy to do in November in Oregon. But this is the next best thing, right? A bedroom right *on* the lake?"

"Next best thing? This is the best thing. I can't believe you did this for me."

"Why not?"

"Well, you're only my fake boyfriend for the week. And—"

"And you're an amazing woman who helped my daughter find some purpose in her life. And you're incredibly beautiful, and I'm having the time of my life with you this week. And if you don't know why a man takes a beautiful woman to a cabin on the lake, then I'm not going to tell you."

"You're trying to get me into bed. It's working."

"Then why aren't you in bed?"

"That," she said, pointing at his chest, "is a very good question. But I have a very good answer."

"What's your very good answer?" he asked as he pulled her into a tight embrace.

"You haven't put me there yet."

"You know what?" he asked.

"What?"

He picked her up off her feet and started to carry her to the bed.

"That *is* a very good answer."

9

ERICK WOULD HAVE patted himself on the back for how well this plan was working out. They'd been at the lake cabin all of five minutes and not only was Clover ready to jump into bed, she was happy. God, that smile of hers... If it were a plant it would be a sunflower. Sunflower? Really? He was turning into Mother Nature's handmaiden. Better than being a drone, right?

"Wait," Clover said. "I forgot something. Put me down."

"Did you leave something at the house?" he asked.

"No, I have it here. I just have to go, um, do something. Do you mind?"

"You're about to have sex with me. Do you think I mind? I wouldn't mind if you stomped on my foot, set the bed on fire and threw me into the lake as long as we got naked after."

She smiled and kissed his cheek. "You have weird sexual fantasies. Put me down. I'll be right back."

He put her down, reluctantly but quickly. She grabbed her overnight bag and raced up the stairs with it. While she was gone doing whatever lady thing she needed to do—shave something or brush something or put perfume on something—he pulled back the covers on the bed and lit the two oil lamps Joey had told him were stored under the kitchen sink.

Man, he was going to owe Chris and Joey for eternity for letting them use this place for free for a couple days. A house like this would rent for four or five hundred a night, easy, during peak season. In addition to the bed in the front room, there were two bedrooms upstairs. The kitchen was exposed brick with stainless-steel appliances but the rest of the house had all the rustic charm one would want from a lake house. Distressed pine floors, carved stair railings, woven rugs and cedar paneling. The chandelier really pulled it all together. From the outside, it looked like a standard crystal light fixture one might find in a hotel lobby. Once inside, however, it revealed its secret. The crystals were actually mason jars of all sizes with LED lights threaded through them. It was a masterpiece of rustic folk art. Steffensen did good work. Just the woodwork alone turned Erick on. Put Clover in that big beautiful bed and he was a goner. An absolute goner. No doubt he loved his daughter more than life itself, but if this was the sort of stuff that happened when she left town, then the first day of college could not come fast enough.

Erick turned off all the lights but the two oil lamps he set on either side of the bed. He stripped out of his clothes and slid between the covers, propped up on thick down pillows to watch absolutely nothing happening out on the lake but the wind on the water. Clover seemed to think that sound was talking to her. Maybe it was talking to him, too, because it seemed a voice whispered in his ear, "Watch out...you're going to fall in love with this woman if you aren't careful..."

Stupid voice. Did it think he didn't know that already? He'd been fighting off a crush on Clover ever since Ruthie went to work for her. Since that kiss yesterday, he'd stopped fighting and let himself feel everything he'd been trying not to feel for Clover for the past year. Instead of ignoring her quiet loveliness, her full lips, her long hair that he'd told himself wouldn't look as good down as he imagined it would, he gave himself full permission to enjoy every glance at her, every kiss, every strand of that sun-colored hair so soft in his fingers. He'd convinced himself she wasn't interested in him because of the wall of professional reserve she'd put up around herself. She'd never once flirted with him during his many trips to the nursery to drop off or pick up Ruthie. Now he knew the reasons for her reserve and could only feel supremely flattered she'd let those walls down with him. And damn, it was beautiful behind those walls. He could live there.

As much as he wanted to tell her that, something held him back. He'd been Clover's first real lover. While he was flattered by that, even a little moved, he also couldn't shake the idea that she would probably prefer to take things slowly with him. What woman wanted to commit herself to the very first guy she slept with? He'd lost his virginity in high school and had two serious girlfriends by the time he met Ruthie's mother, got her pregnant—a happy accident—and had Ruthie. Wouldn't Clover want to explore her options, date around, enjoy her newfound sexual confidence a little bit before committing to a serious relationship? Probably. He would in her shoes.

The other voice in his head sounded suspiciously like Ruthie's and that voice was telling him that he should let Clover take the lead, let her decide what sort of relationship she wanted. That was a fair point. He'd leave it to Clover, then. If she told him she wanted to keep seeing him, then he'd tell her how crazy about her he was. If he told her today, she might feel pressured to commit before she was ready and that's the last thing he wanted her to do. Bad enough she had her entire family trying to force her to get married and have kids. He wasn't about to add to the chorus of voices nagging her about her personal life.

Therefore, it was decided. For Clover's sake he'd keep his runaway feelings to himself for the time being. He'd enjoy this week with Clover and give her the best nights of her life if he could. If they only had the one week together, it was better than nothing. If it was the beginning of something real, even better. Much, much better.

Now that he'd had this little talk with himself and adjusted his romantic expectations, Erick closed his eyes and felt at peace with the universe—calm, relaxed and happy.

"You're smiling," Clover said. He smiled wider.

"I am."

"Do I want to know why?"

"Just happy," he said. "Where are you?"

"On the stairs. I'm coming down. Just stay there."

"I'm naked. I'm not going anywhere."

"Good," she said. "Because you're exactly where I want you."

"And I'm exactly where I want to be."

"Really?"

Erick opened his eyes and found Clover standing by the side of the bed.

In the ten minutes she'd been gone in the bathroom upstairs, she had transformed herself from her usual natural beauty in jeans, turtleneck and a fleece pull-over to a goddess in white lingerie. She wore a white lace-and-silk gown that clung to her every curve and stopped at the top of her thighs, with matching white lace panties underneath. She'd taken her hair out of her usual standard-issue ponytail, parted it down the center and curled it so that it lay in soft waves past her shoulders. He couldn't think of a word to describe her. Even the word *beautiful* seemed inadequate in her presence. Exquisite? Elegant? A goddess? He'd go with that one.

"You look like a goddess," he said.

"I feel ridiculous. Like it?"

He took her by the hand and pulled her down gently to the bed. He kissed her, pushed her onto her back on the sheets and slid on top of her, nothing between them but lace.

"I don't like it at all," he said, pushing his erection into her. "I love it. When did you buy this?" He hoped she'd say today, that she bought it just for him, but he had a feeling that wasn't the case.

"After my surgery I went on a shopping spree." She wrapped her arms around his shoulders and he kissed her neck. "I bought something I couldn't wear before when my breasts were too big. This is it. It's been in the back of my closet since then."

"You've never worn this before?"

"Never."

"You got it out for me?"

"I couldn't think of anyone else I'd make myself this ridiculous for."

"You…" He tapped the end of her nose. "You have a strange idea of 'ridiculous.' Why do you feel ridiculous?"

"I'm just not a lingerie type. I'm a six-pack of cotton underwear from Target kind of gal."

"You'd be beautiful in a burlap bag, but you are insanely beautiful in lingerie. You might feel ridiculous but you don't look ridiculous. And you shouldn't feel ridiculous dressing up or down for me. It's what lovers do."

"You'd put on lingerie for me?"

"I'd put anything on for you that you wanted. Name it. If they make it in my size, I'll wear it if it turns you on."

"You're wearing my favorite of all your looks right now."

"It is pretty comfortable," he said. "You could wear this, too." He slipped his fingers under the strap of her gown and slowly pulled it down her arm.

"Oh, no," she said. "I worked up the courage to put this thing on for you. I'm not about to let you take it off me until I get some use out of it."

"How long do I have to leave it on you?"

"Hmm…" She pursed her lips, tapped her chin, and looked so adorable he couldn't stand it. "One hour."

He turned his head and checked the cuckoo clock on the wall.

"It's eighty thirty-five. By nine thirty-five I get to take this off you?"

She nodded. "In the meantime we have to find things to do that don't involve me being naked. Any ideas?" she asked.

"One or two or a million. Let's start with this one."

He moved onto his side and put his hand under her gown, resting it on her stomach. He kissed her hard and heavily, mingling their tongues together as he cupped her between her legs with his palm. For a long time he did nothing but kiss her and press his hand gently and rhythmically against her. Her body warmed to his touch and her panties grew damp as he teased her through the thin lace. If she wanted to torture him by keeping her clothes on for a full hour, he would find a way to torture her back in the sweetest ways possible.

He lowered his head and kissed her breasts through the fabric of her gown, blowing hot air on her nipples and watching them harden through the silk. He kissed the soft tops of her breasts as he made tiny circles around her swollen clitoris with his fingertip. Clover's chest rose and fell over and over with her shallow breaths. He glanced up once to look at her and saw her head lying back on the pillow, her eyes closed. She was the very picture of a woman lost in erotic pleasure. As much as he wanted to be inside her, Erick also wanted to make her come first to prove to her that a little slip of silk and lace wasn't about to get in his way. Through the silk he sucked on her nipple while pulling the fabric of her panties to the side.

"You're soaking wet," he said into her ear. "Did you know that?"

"I assumed so… I mean, you're here, so of course I am."

"Of course you are." He felt inordinate male pride at her words. Of course she was wet. He was there. Of course…

"That explains why I'm rock hard," he said. "You're here."

"I love it when you're hard."

"I love it when you're here."

She looked at him through eyes half-closed in ecstasy and smiled. Such a smile should have gone straight to his groin. But instead he felt that smile in his heart. He cared for this woman, already. Before this week he'd adored her for what she'd done for his daughter. Now he simply adored her. And it was on the tip of his tongue to tell her that when Clover raised her hips imploringly and whispered a soft "Please…"

He pushed his finger inside her and her head fell back on the bed again. A whole hour before he could strip her naked and fuck her like he needed to…a whole hour… He could spend half of it doing just this, massaging her inside. Her vagina was hot to the touch, slick with her arousal. He slid his finger up the front wall, watching her face the entire time, looking for hints of pleasure or displeasure. He wanted to know what made her tick, what felt good to her, what didn't. He wanted to know her inside and out but right now the inside of her was his top priority.

He felt a soft hollow and pushed his fingertip into it. Clover inhaled sharply and he caught the ghost of a smile on her lips. He did it again and she inhaled again. He pushed a second finger into her and she opened her legs wider to give him more room to move in her. It was such a simple thing, spreading for him, and yet it drove him wild with desire and need. Did Clover have any idea how sexy she was like this—spread out under his hand, wet and hot and open to him and for him?

"I love it when you spread for me," he whispered in her ear. She shivered at his words. "It's killing me not to fuck you right now." He rubbed that soft hollow with his fingertips.

"It won't kill you."

"It might kill me. But what a way to go."

She grinned with her eyes closed. He rubbed her a little harder, made the circle a little larger. The grin disappeared.

"Erick—" She gasped his name and it was the sexiest word she could have spoken right then.

"I want you to come on my fingers. Will you do that for me?" he asked. "Pretty please…"

She gave a low sexy laugh. "As long as you keep doing that I will. Promise."

"I wouldn't stop fucking you with my fingers if the world ended outside this house. Take your time to come for me, but when you come, come hard."

Erick wanted her to come but he was in no hurry to stop. He moved in and out of her with his fingers, stroking them along her inner walls, going deep before settling in again in that spot that made her so breathless when he touched it. At first he touched and massaged it gently and slowly, but as Clover's shallow breaths turned into soft moans, he rubbed hard and pushed deeper into that spot, deeper and harder, harder and deeper. Clover opened her thighs even wider and pumped her hips into his hand and it was so sexy he could have come from watching her alone. A million erotic fantasies ran through his mind as he fucked her with his fingers. He wanted to rip her panties off, flip her onto her hands and knees and ram his cock into her from behind. He wanted to brace her against the wall, fucking her with her legs wrapped around him. He wanted to eat her pussy until she screamed. He wanted her mouth wrapped around his cock as he came deep in her throat. He wanted to spend the rest of his life inside her body.

The rest of his life?

Clover gasped his name again and her shoulders came off the bed as she came with an orgasm so powerful he could feel every muscle inside her gripping his fingers. Wetness poured out of her and onto the sheets underneath. Involuntarily her legs closed, trapping his hand inside her, which he didn't mind one bit.

"Good girl..." He kissed her on the lips. She didn't return the kiss but he took that as a compliment. If he'd come as hard as she just had, he'd need a minute or more to recover, too.

"Good girl?" she panted. "Not bad girl?"

"There's nothing bad about what we just did," he said.

"Feels so wicked."

"Good wicked."

"Wicked good."

"That's it," he said, kissing her again, and this time she returned the kiss with equal ardor.

"That was incredible," she said as she lowered her head back to the bed. "I didn't know my body could do that."

"It was pretty incredible. But I do have one question for you."

"Ask me anything."

"Are you going to give me my hand back?"

She looked down where his hand was still trapped between her thighs, his fingers still inside her.

"No," she said.

"That's fine. It's better off where it is."

Laughing sheepishly, she spread her legs again and Erick slipped his fingers out of her.

He glanced over his shoulder at the cuckoo clock on the wall again.

"Only nine," he said. "What are we going to do for another thirty-five minutes?"

"I have an idea."

"Does it involve my cock?"

"It does."

"Say no more. I'm already sold on this idea."

"I can't say any more about it."

"Why not?"

"Because," she said as she pushed him onto his back and straddled his thighs, "my mouth is full."

She lowered her head and licked him from the base of his cock to the head. He groaned and she giggled and it was the sweetest combination of sounds he'd ever heard. This woman…this incredible woman…so innocent, so erotic, and all at once. Where had she been all of his life? Oh, yeah, right there, under his nose.

Clover looked up at him with an expectant expression on her face.

"Tell me what you like," she said.

"But I'm shy."

"You are such a liar." She shook her head. God, he loved driving this woman crazy.

"I can't help it. You're so cute when you're annoyed with me."

"You are not shy. You are the least shy man I've ever met."

"That's probably true." He nodded.

"It is true. Now tell me what you like. I know you're going to do it, anyway, at some point."

"Also true. Okay…" He took her by the wrist and placed her hand on him. "Rub first with your hand. Kind of pull, but gently. No pulling it off."

"No pulling it off. Good tip."

She did as he instructed, and it was as much a pleasure to watch as it was to feel. Erick put a pillow behind his head, propping himself up enough that he could watch her as she worked.

"Is this good?" she asked as she ran her hand over him, lightly pulling, lightly caressing.

"It's perfect. Oral is a lot of stimulation. I need to warm up for it or it'll be too much all at once."

"I'm making mental notes of all of this," she said. "I like hearing what works for you. It's sexy."

"It's good you like hearing it because we both know I can't shut up when my cock's hard."

"I've never had anyone talk to me like you do. I didn't think it would be as sexy as it is, but…it is."

He reached down and caressed her cheek and lips.

"You bring out the horny poet in me."

"What do I do now, horny poet?"

"Lick," he said. "Just lick."

She lowered her head again and licked him from base to tip, from tip to base. Every lick kicked his temperature up a degree. Watching her as she did it kicked it up another. That pink tongue of hers, those pale pink lips…so sweet, just like candy. He couldn't wait to see them all red and swollen after she sucked him off.

And he told her that.

"Dirty mouth," she said.

"Guilty."

"I'd smile but my mouth's a little too busy," she said as she licked him again.

"Suck the head now. Smile later."

She took direction well, that was for sure. Him telling her exactly what to do seemed to help with her confidence. When he told her to increase the pressure with her hand, she did. When he told her to run her tongue around the rim of his cock, she did—twice. When he told her to take as much of it as she could into her mouth and suck hard and deep, she did it over and over again until he couldn't tell her what to do any longer.

Instinct must have taken over because she put her hand on the shaft and stroked it while she sucked the head and licked it. He managed to whisper a desperate "That…keep doing that…" before he lost all pow-

ers of speech and could do nothing but moan and gasp.
It was ecstasy, pure erotic ecstasy. He reached down
and put his hands on Clover's back, rubbing her shoulders and caressing her hair as she went down on him,
sucking and licking him and making him feel like a
god. He had to touch her. The most beautiful woman
in the world doing the sexiest act in the world in the
most beautiful cabin on the most beautiful lake in the
most beautiful forest in the entire universe...he was the
luckiest man alive.

Erick dug his heels into the bed and felt all the
muscles in his legs and back locking up as he neared
orgasm. With his eyes shut tight he breathed as de-
liberately as he could, hoping to prolong this incredible pleasure for a second or two more. But it just felt
too good. He couldn't hold back. The need to come
was overwhelming. He'd die if he didn't come. Clover
held all the power in that moment. With his cock in
her mouth, she owned him. She owned him body and
soul. He would have begged her to let him come if she'd
made him, begged her with pleasure and no pride at all.
Maybe he was begging. God only knew what was coming out of his mouth right now...

When his need to release was at its strongest, its most
desperate, he felt it starting to explode out of him. He
came hard into Clover's warm soft mouth, waves of
pleasure rolling through him and out of him. His stomach muscles tightened and released and his hips jerked
as a spasm of sharp pleasure shot through him. His orgasm seemed to go on forever but was over in seconds.
He collapsed back onto the pillow, empty and sated and
happy, his hair plastered with sweat to his forehead and
every muscle in his body slack.

He felt Clover leave the bed but he didn't worry about

it. She might have gone to spit and he couldn't blame her if she did. She returned quickly with a cup of water and a small wet towel in her hand.

"Lavender wipe?" she offered.

"Ruthie's got you hooked on these, too?" He took the towel from her and wiped off his face.

"They're supposed to be calming. I ordered a whole case of them when I found out my family was coming for Thanksgiving." She drank from her cup and handed it to him. He swallowed the water greedily, grateful for it. His mouth was dry from all the heavy breathing.

"You're too good to me," he said. "Water and lavender wipes and a blow job. I feel spoiled."

"Good to you?" she asked as she sat by him on the edge of the bed. "I enjoyed that. All of that."

"I'm sorry I didn't warn you I was about to come. I know it's kind of a lot to take in."

"You warned me. I didn't mind."

"I did warn you?"

She nodded. "In the midst of telling me all the things you wanted to do to my body and a few things you wanted me to do with yours, you warned me."

"I have postorgasm amnesia. I say this stuff and don't even realize I'm saying it. I hope none of it offended you."

"It didn't. Although some of it's probably impossible. I don't think I can bend that way. And I'm pretty sure one of your suggestions is illegal."

"Illegal?"

"Last I checked, indecent exposure is still a crime in Oregon."

He rolled his eyes. "Clearly you've never been to Portland during the annual Naked Bike Ride."

"I knew I lived an hour from that city for a reason."

She bent and kissed him on the center of his chest. He didn't know why she did that but he liked it. "I did enjoy that. My first full blow job. Very exciting."

"You're good at it."

"You told me exactly what to do. You're a very good teacher."

"You get an A in BJs." He glanced over at the clock and back at her. "It's 9:35. Lose the lace, toots."

"A deal is a deal," she said. Clover stood up and shimmied out of her gown and pulled her panties off. Her naked body glowed in the light of the bedside oil lamp and he couldn't tear his eyes from her full round breasts and the little patch of hair between her legs, nearly as soft and pale as the hair on her head. "Happy now?"

"You are naked. I am the happiest man on earth. Are you the happiest woman on earth?"

"I think so. I mean, I can't guarantee that," she said as she sat on the bed next to him again. "I don't know the happiness quotient of every other woman on earth at the moment, but I'd guess I'm in the top ten at least."

"Ruthie said I can't speak to her again until I've made you the happiest woman on earth."

"You can call your daughter. I'll vouch for you."

"I'll call her tomorrow. Now I'm going to put you in bed next to me and sleep for fifteen minutes. Then I'm going to wake up and fuck you. If you don't mind."

"I don't mind at all. Only fifteen minutes?"

"Hmm…good point. After that orgasm, we better make it thirty minutes."

"I'll be here when you wake up," she said, and it was the sweetest thing she could have said to him. He held her against him, and she rested her head over his heart. Was she thinking what he was thinking? That he

wanted her to be there when he woke up, every time he
woke up, forever? He tried to tell himself he was going
too fast, feeling too much, rushing into things he should
be tiptoeing into. But it wasn't like they were strang-
ers. He'd known her a year. They'd had more than one
long serious talk about Ruthie and her situation after
Clover had hired her. He'd gotten to know her well as
his daughter's boss and as a businesswoman. He trusted
her with his kid, and if that wasn't a sign that they
were good together, he didn't know what was. But this
week, it was just about the two of them. No work. No
Ruthie. Just him, just Clover, just them together. They
were attracted to each other and the sex was incredible.
Ruthie had already given her blessing—sort of. As long
as he took good care of Clover and made her happy,
Ruthie would give her blessing. And it seemed Clover
was having as much fun this week with him as he was
with her. If they could make it through Thanksgiving
without him telling her family they were assholes to
their faces, maybe he had a good shot at making this,
whatever this was, into the real deal.

"Can I ask a girl question?" Clover said.

"I'm not a girl."

"Okay, can I ask a girlie question?"

"You can ask me anything."

"What are you thinking?"

"Why do you ask?"

"You were smiling. I wanted to know what was making you smile."

Erick wanted to tell her the truth, that he was thinking about how good they were together, how much
he cared about her already and how much he hoped
this was going somewhere past Thanksgiving. But he
didn't say that because Ruthie had trained him too well.

He knew better than to put that kind of pressure on a woman this early in a relationship. So he told her a half-truth.

"I'm thinking I'm very glad you picked me over Sven."

10

"Parents?" Clover asked. "I assume you have them?"

"I do. And they're both still alive and kicking. Mom works at the post office and Dad's a roofer. He's slowed down a little the past few years but he still works more than he needs to."

"Siblings?"

"Only child. My parents like to say they got it right the first time."

"Um…" She paused and tried to think of the sorts of things her family would bring up at Thanksgiving dinner. "Concerts?" Clover asked. "That might come up in conversation. Hunter and Lisa go to a lot of concerts. He's on the local symphony's board of directors."

"Last concert I went to was a couple years ago when Ruthie was going through an obsessed with Haim phase. Great show."

"Concerts you wanted to go to."

"I've seen DMB live five times," Erick said. "But all in high school."

Clover nodded. "So, you were a stoner in high school, I see."

"I wish," he said. "But nope. I really don't have an excuse. I legitimately loved their music."

Clover smiled behind her coffee cup as Erick resumed his rowing. The weather had turned vaguely pleasant, at least for late November in Oregon. The sky was steel gray with clouds but it wasn't raining and the temperature had hovered near sixty since noon. Perfect weather for taking a boat out onto the lake. Erick had insisted on rowing and she didn't mind at all, sitting back and watching him work. He wore a lightweight black sweater with the sleeves shoved up to his elbows, which gave her a glorious view of his muscular forearms as he pulled back on the oars. She knew she should be checking out the scenery—the mountain, the trees, the lake—but Erick was without a doubt the best part of her view.

"What about you?" he asked. "Concerts? Favorite bands?"

"I played cello in high school and college. I'm still kind of a classical music snob. But I love Alison Krauss, too."

"Country, right?"

"Bluegrass and country. Mom's an English professor so books will probably come up in conversation. Favorite books? Last book read?" Clover asked.

"Last book read was Bill Bryson's *A Walk in the Woods*. Favorite book? Either *A Farewell to Arms* or *House Made of Dawn*."

"I've never read either of those."

"Ruthie had to read them in her AP Lit classes. I'd read Hemingway a little in high school but read him again when she did. I'd never read *House*, either, but whew, damn good stuff."

"You read what Ruthie reads in school?"

"Why not? I mean, I know she's smarter than me, but I'm not about to let her figure that out yet."

"She is smart, but so is her father."

"Tell her that."

"I will. She might be able to name the ritual healing properties of a hundred different kinds of incense but I highly doubt she knows how to build a cedar deck."

"Yeah, she doesn't go near cedar. She says it has too many masculine properties. Supposedly the scent of it increases male virility."

"That explains last night. And this morning."

"And tonight and tomorrow morning…"

She leaned forward and kissed him on the forward motion of his rowing.

"I completely forgot what we were talking about," he said when he pulled back on the oars again.

"We were talking about how wood gives you wood."

"Before that."

"Books and music and other stuff real couples know about each other so we can trick my family into thinking we've been dating longer than three days," Clover said, tensing at the thought of Thanksgiving. Two days. Only two days away. She wished it was today to get it over with. She wished it was a year away so she had more time with Erick.

"Where's your family from?" Erick asked. "Where did you grow up? I should probably know something about your past. That might come up."

"Born and raised in Redmond. After Mom got her PhD, they moved to Sacramento and she started teaching at CSU. She retired last year. I was in college when they moved so I stayed in Oregon. Hunter's my older brother. He's a bank manager in Spokane. My sister got married right out of college to the son of a Seattle real estate developer."

"That sounds like money."

"A lot of money. Kelly has never had to work, which is why she has four kids already even though she's eighteen months younger than I am."

"Four kids? At twenty-eight?"

"One set of twins—Ian and Eva. The oldest is Elena. Gus is the baby. He just turned four. Hunter's married to Lisa and they have three girls—Skye, Paige and Zoe. All spelled with *e*'s. Got all that?"

Erick blew a hard breath and his eyes went wide. "I need to write this stuff down. Can I get a chart or something?"

"I'll make you a spreadsheet."

"Thank you. And maybe flash cards. What about your dad?"

"He's also an academic. Retired associate dean of Sacramento State. That's another issue with my family. I went to college for three years but dropped out before graduating."

"Why'd you drop out?"

"I got offered a very good job at the nursery I worked at part-time. Management position, good pay and benefits. I was so much happier at work than at school, I took the job. With a professor mother and a dean father? That didn't go over so well."

"I can see them not being happy about it then, but it's not like you're a burnout selling pencils on the street and sleeping in gutters. You've done pretty well for yourself."

"Tell them that," she said. "I mean, don't tell them that. We aren't going to fight with my family. We are going to suck it up and get through it without anyone losing it. Especially me."

"If you say so. Are you sure you want to do this? I can pretend to have hep A or something."

"There's an idea. The good news about my family is that the kids are all great. Very sweet and well behaved. Them, I really want to see. I might even eat at the kids' table." Clover wasn't kidding. She'd survived many a family meal by using the kids as human shields. Nobody would ask her about her personal life while she was playing tea party with her nieces.

"So let me get this straight—your parents have seven grandkids already, and they're still bugging you to get married and have kids? Aren't they being a little greedy? My parents have one grandkid. One. And they said that's plenty."

"Seven. And that's apparently not enough for them, so at least pretend you want more kids even if you don't. It'll shut them up."

"I'll mention the thing about cedar and male virility. 'Want some pumpkin pie? Also my sperm count is probably really high because I work with cedar.' How's that?"

"Sounds perfect. Thanksgiving is going to be a blast."

"You said that while looking at the peak of Mount Hood."

"Are we one hundred percent certain that Mount Hood isn't going to explode this week?" she asked. "Just a tiny eruption would work. I'm sure they'd make us evacuate."

"Not going to erupt. All my fault. I sacrificed a virgin to it this week. It's appeased," Erick said.

Clover sighed. "There's never a volcano eruption when you need one."

She stared out at the water and inhaled the crisp autumn air. She should have felt peaceful out here on the lake with the water gently slapping the side of the blue aluminum boat and the snowcapped peak of Mount Hood looming over Erick's shoulder and the Canada geese flying overhead in a halfhearted V formation. She even spied a majestic bald eagle in the bare branches of a vine maple and heard the unmistakable rat-a-tat-tat of a woodpecker close by. But as sublime and tranquil as the setting was, she couldn't relax completely even for Erick's sake. Especially for Erick's sake. Three days ago she would have said she asked Erick to play fake boyfriend on Thanksgiving because her family would approve. Responsible single father, small-business owner, handsome and sweet and funny. A perfect fake boyfriend, right? Except her mother had decided Erick was a bad match for Clover for the sole reason he had an almost-adult daughter and would surely not want more kids. Once her mother got something into her head, there was no getting it out again. And if her mom or her dad said something rude to Erick or about Erick… Clover didn't even want to think about it. Mount Hood would have nothing on her eruption if her parents said something rude to Erick. But surely they wouldn't, not with their middle child and favorite bull's-eye there to take the darts.

"You're very stressed out about Thursday, aren't you?" Erick asked.

"I'm considering throwing myself in this lake in the hopes I'll get bitten by a piranha and will have to spend a few days in the hospital."

"You know there are no piranhas in Lost Lake, right?"

"What about sharks?"

"It's going to be fine," Erick said as he turned the boat to steer it away from a submerged tree. "It'll be over before you know it. They'll show up, you'll introduce me to everyone, we'll stick close to each other, we'll eat, we'll have a couple glasses of wine, we'll have dessert and then we'll do that thing where we serve coffee so people know it's time for them to leave. Then poof—" He blew on his fingers. "They'll be gone."

"That's why people serve coffee at parties? To get their guests to leave?"

Erick nodded. "Best trick in the book. It's a subtle way of saying, 'Wake up and go away, please.'"

"Coffee. Good idea."

"What is it you're so worried about? What do you think's going to happen?"

Clover shrugged and shook her head.

"I think they're going to be mean to you."

Erick burst into laughter, and the sound bounced off the water and echoed into the trees.

"Mean to me? You're worried they're going to be mean to me? Like 'punch me in the face and call me Shorty' mean? 'Shove me into lockers and steal my lunch money' mean? I'm a grown man, Clover. What could they do to me? Give me a wedgie? I've survived worse."

"Well, no. They're not going to be mean like that. They're just kind of snobby sometimes."

"Ah. And I do manual labor for a living. But so do you."

"Yeah, and they're rude to me about it."

"What do they say to you?"

"Mom says I'll wreck my back by doing so much

gardening and it'll make it hard for me to pick up my children."

"You don't have children."

"Not yet, but she's planning on it already. She says I should get an MBA like Hunter did since I'm business-minded. I could teach instead of ruining my body with all this physical labor I'm doing."

"I've seen your body. If that's what ruined looks like, sign me up for ruination."

"Meanwhile Kelly says my life is so much easier than hers because she has to keep her kids alive whereas no-body cares if plants die. And Dad has said repeatedly I should have been a botanist."

"Is that bad? Suggesting you should have been a botanist?"

"It's bad when 'You should be a botanist' is followed by 'instead of working retail.'"

"Working retail? Shit, that's what they think you do?"

"I ring up customers sometimes when they buy my plants at the nursery. Ergo, I'm working retail. That I own the business doesn't seem to compute with Dad."

"Wow. Your family is a bunch of snobs, aren't they?"

"The worst part is that they don't even know they're doing it. So you can't call them out on it because it just won't register. I once told my sister, 'Please don't act like my work is unimportant just because you don't care about plants.' And she said, 'Oh, Clover, don't be ridiculous. I think your work sounds so fun.'"

"Fun. But not important."

"They hear what they want to hear. And there's not much I can do about it except grin and bear it and then go back to my happy and busy life until the next holi-day when I make myself grin and bear it again. This is why April through September is my favorite time of the year—it's the busiest time at the nursery and no major holidays."

"Maybe Ruthie and I will kidnap you at Christmas so you can have an excuse to avoid your family."

"It would be a Christmas miracle." She sighed wistfully, imagining the happy thought of Erick and Ruthie dragging her out of her family's Christmas party and throwing her in the back of a white van.

"We'll see about making that happen. Ruthie's been dying to commit another felony, anyway, before she turns eighteen. Kidnapping you sounds fun. I might tie you to the bed with a big red bow."

"Finally, a reason to look forward to a holiday."

"You know, your family can be as mean to me as they want. They're not my family. I won't give a damn about what they say. No skin off my nose."

"My siblings aren't that bad but my parents will find a way to needle you. Trust me."

"They can try. I'm impervious to needling. I have a teenage daughter. You grow very thick skin when you have a teenage daughter as intelligent as mine."

"Is Ruthie mean to you?"

"Vicious. She said I wasn't good enough for you."

"What?" Clover nearly fell out of the boat.

"If you ever wondered why I call her Ruthless...that's why. Because she is."

"Surely she didn't mean that."

"She did. But it's not because she thinks I'm a bad person. She thinks you're too good for almost anybody out there."

"That's very sweet of her. Even when she's trying to be mean she's sweet. Which is kind of the opposite of my parents, who are mean even when they're trying to be sweet."

"Ruthie is not passive-aggressive. She's just *aggressive*-aggressive."

"And I'm passive-passive. Must be why Ruthie and I get along so well. Unless I catch her insulting you again. Then I'll show her how mean I can be."

"Not mean at all, you mean."

"Yeah, I'm a wimp."

"You are not a wimp. It takes a very strong person to tolerate a family like that without going off on them. I think you should go off on them, but that's just what I would do."

"Don't, please. You're a wonderful man and I know you'll want to defend me when they say stuff to me—and they will—but please don't fight back. I'll never hear the end of it from them. I told you I quit college to take a good job. Nine years ago that happened. Nine years. You know what they still call me? I'm their 'little dropout.' And I bet you money they'll call me that in front of you."

"Are you sure I can't go off on them?"

"I'm sure. I think."

"Are you sure you're sure?"

"I'm sure I'm sure. Erick… I like you."

"Oh, stop." He batted his eyelashes.

"You stop. I mean, I really like you. I'd like to keep seeing you if I can. If you want. If you like that idea. No pressure."

"Clover, I've spent the last three days having the best sex of my life with the most beautiful woman I've ever dated. I think it's safe to say I like the idea of us seeing each other even after Thanksgiving."

"Good," she said. "I'm glad to hear it. But I'm serious here, if you go off on my family, they will shun you. I have a cousin my mother hasn't spoken to in three years because he dared suggest their darling son-in-law, Mike, the Seattle real estate developer, was doing the city more harm than good with all his gentrification projects. If you and I are maybe going to keep seeing each other—"

"No maybe. Definitely not a maybe."

She grinned. "*Since* we're going to keep seeing each other, I'd like us to stay on their good side. That's all. We just have to get through Thanksgiving without losing our tempers with them. Otherwise I will truly never ever hear the end of it for as long as I live. And it's not worth it to me. Understand?"

"I understand. I don't like it, but I understand."

"Thank you. Now let's do something other than talk about my family."

"It's really a boner killer."

"Sorry. What's the opposite of a boner killer?"

"You."

"You want to talk about me?"

"I would love to talk about you. I would love to talk about you in bed."

"We're in a boat. No bed here, and the cabin is way over there." She pointed to a tiny speck in the distance. Erick had rowed them all the way from one side of Lost Lake to the other. Now they had to row back.

"I can get us back there in no time."

"It took us two hours to get out here."

"Give me some inspiration."

"Hmm…how about this? As soon as we get back to the cabin, I'll do that thing you suggested we do while I was going down on you last night."

"I don't remember what I said. I was in a sex trance."

"Then let's get back to the cabin and I'll tell you what you said. Then we'll do it."

"You drive a hard bargain. And by that I mean I'm hard."

"Start rowing, mister."

Erick rowed them halfway back to the cabin, then stopped in the middle of the lake.

"What's wrong?" Clover asked.

"I just remembered something," he said.

"What?"

"I'm old."

"You rest. I'll row," she said, taking the oars from him.

"Or we could fuck in the boat."

"I'm not putting my bare ass on an aluminum boat bottom," she said. "It's too cold to have sex outside."

"Not even oral?"

"There is a man and his two sons on the shore fishing right over there."

"So that's a no to boat oral?"

"That is a no to boat oral."

"Give me those oars," he said.

Clover refused and she started rowing the boat back to the cabin. She wasn't as fast as Erick but slow and steady wins the race, and with sex being the prize for this race, she rowed, certain of victory.

"Ruthie would be proud of me for letting you row," he said. "Men are supposed to be willing to give up the reins in a relationship. I guess oars are similar to reins. We'll pretend they are."

"Do I have the reins in this relationship, then?"

"Absolutely. Your wish is my command. Command me."

"Here's a serious command. I need to figure out what to do with the nursery so I command you to help me."

"What to do about it?" he asked. "What's the problem with it? I thought you were going gangbusters."

"We are. That's the problem. PNW Garden Supply wants to buy us."

"For how much?"

"Five?"

"Five hundred thousand?"

"Five million."

Erick's eyes went wide, his mouth dropped open. It was the reaction she was hoping for. "Holy shit."

"Yeah, that was what I said. But we've been turning big profits the last two years. I invested it all back into the company after putting a chunk in my retirement account. Five million's a good offer but reasonable for what the nursery's two locations pull in."

"Too reasonable? You want them to up their offer?"

"They already upped from four-point-five. The price is good. I'm not going to haggle. What's hard is figuring out if I want to sell or not at any price."

"That is a hard decision, but whatever you go with, that's pretty incredible. I'm so proud of you. I'd high-five you but my palms are bleeding."

The left oar fell out of Clover's hand and she nearly dumped the boat over while retrieving it from the lake.

"Crap, sorry," she said, fishing the oar from the water.

"Hey, you okay there?" Erick asked as he dragged her back into the boat. She'd gotten her sleeves wet but that was the extent of the damage. "Clover? Babe, what's wrong?"

She swallowed hard and smiled at him, feeling incredibly pitiful and yet happy at the same time.

"Nothing," she said softly. "Nothing's wrong."

"You're crying. Something is wrong. Are you sad about maybe selling the business? I would be. You put a lot of work into it. It's kind of your baby except the sort of baby you can legally sell."

"It's not that. It isn't. I can start a new business. It's just…"

"What?"

"You're the first person in my life who's ever said that to me about the nursery."

"Said what?"

"That you're proud of me." Two hot fat tears rolled out of her eyes and down her cheeks. Hastily she wiped them off.

"Clover… I didn't mean to make you cry. It's a dad thing, saying, 'I'm proud of you.' Can't help it."

"It is a dad thing. But Dad never said that to me. You said it to me. The guy I've been dating for three days said it to me, but my own parents who have known me for thirty years haven't. Not once. Never a single, 'Wow, you know, Clover, we were disappointed when you quit school but you really proved us wrong. We're proud of your success. Great job.' It just meant a lot to hear that from you."

"I am proud of you. You started this business only five years ago and you're already getting a multimillion-dollar buyout offer from a competitor? That's something to be proud of."

"It is. It really is. I just wish they would…you know, give a damn about something other than my personal life. It's like nothing I do matters if I'm not married and breeding. And if I'm not married and breeding, at least I could be doing something respectable like teaching. Something that doesn't involve dirt, worms and blisters."

"You don't need your parents to tell you they're proud of you. You know why?"

"Because you're proud of me?"

"Because you're proud of yourself. Aren't you?"

"Well..."

"Aren't you, Clover? I would be. I'd have already called every person in my phone to crow about it. You are allowed to be proud of yourself."

"I am proud of myself."

"Hell, yes, you are."

He held out his hand for her to slap it in a high five, and she saw he hadn't been kidding about his bleeding palms. He had a blister on his hand that had broken open.

"Oh, my God, Erick. You really are horny."

"It's fine. One blister. Put a little alcohol on it and a Band-Aid and I'll be good to go."

"How's your other hand?"

"Don't look. Please. I'm trying to get laid here."

"You're still going to get laid. The thing you suggested we do last night doesn't require hands. Well, it doesn't require your hands. Your hands are supposed to be tied up to the bedpost."

"Row faster, Clover. Row like the wind."

Clover had never rowed faster in her life.

11

ERICK WOKE UP on Wednesday morning to the prettiest sight he'd ever seen in his life. The first hints of dawn had started peeking over the trees and spreading sunlight across the lake. And there was Clover, her pale hair down and around her shoulders, kneeling on the edge of the bed with a white sheet wrapped around her, watching the sunrise through the wall of windows in front of their bed. As she watched the sunrise, he watched her.

A long slant of light slid across the dock and slipped into the bottom set of windows. The white sheets turned gold, and like a cat, Clover stretched out into the light, lying on her side and facing the lake. Erick crawled over to her and without a word spooned up behind her, kissing her naked neck and shoulders. They were leaving the cabin in a couple hours so they should make the most of the bed and the view and each other while they could.

"You're in the manly way again," Clover said.

"Am I? Sorry. It's all the cedar," he said, and she chuckled.

She started to roll over to face him and he stopped her with a hand on her hip.

"Stay where you are," he said. "Don't miss the sunrise. First good one we've had all week."

Clover stayed on her side facing the windows and Erick kept kissing her back and running his fingers through her hair. No doubt about it, he was hopelessly addicted to this woman. He'd been relieved to an embarrassing degree yesterday when Clover said she wanted to keep seeing him after this week. He congratulated himself on playing it cool, but he'd been dancing with happiness on the inside. As long as he could get through Thanksgiving without doing something spectacularly stupid like calling all her immediate family assholes to their faces, they could maybe, just maybe, have something very special here.

Erick ran his hand over Clover's soft stomach and her hips and thighs. She breathed softly and with pleasure at his touch. He'd done everything he could to help her make up for lost time this week. There wasn't an inch of her body he hadn't touched or kissed, a sexual position they hadn't at least attempted or a fantasy they hadn't talked about. He couldn't believe she'd actually tied his hands to the bed yesterday after they got back from rowing. Most women he'd dated had been uncomfortable with that sort of thing, which he told Clover. She'd replied, saying, "How will I know if I like it or not unless I try it at least once?" And since he didn't have a good answer to that question, they'd blissfully decided to try it all.

But this morning all he wanted to do was make love to her while the sun rose and the lake woke up all around them. He lifted Clover's leg and draped it back over his thigh. With his fingers he tested her wetness, making sure she was ready for him. They'd had sex late last night and she still felt damp and open. She took his fingers inside her easily and with a soft moan of pleasure. He rubbed the head of his cock against her outer lips as he teased her clitoris with his fingers. Just as the sun flooded the room with light, he entered her deeply and with a long slow thrust.

He groaned as he went into her. Her heat was pure bliss wrapped around his cock. In this position he couldn't thrust hard or fast, which was fine by him. He thrust gently and leisurely instead, taking all the time in the world because he could do this the rest of his life as long as it was with Clover.

"You're so hot inside," he whispered into her ear between sucks and nibbles on her earlobe. "I love your pussy."

"It loves you," she said.

He slid his other arm under and around her and took both of her breasts in his hands and squeezed them as he pumped his hips into her. Clover moaned, arching her back to take more of him. Erick loved how much she loved his cock and wasn't afraid to show it and say it and enjoy every inch of it. As the sun showed its full face over the top of the tree line and the glorious peak of Mount Hood glowed in the distance, Erick rolled onto his back, dragging Clover with him and on top of him. He licked his two fingers and rubbed her where they joined. She was so wet, wet and swollen, swollen and throbbing. With his other hand he pinched her nipples lightly, caressed them, pulled them, anything to keep Clover breathing like that, like she was on the edge of coming and wanted to live on that edge. They both were at the edge of something terrifying and beautiful like that ancient active volcanic peak rising up over the lake. Erick rolled his pelvis to deepen the penetration and Clover gasped, a sound of unbridled ecstasy. He felt her orgasm on his fingertips as a thousand nerve endings exploded all at once. Hearing it and feeling it was too much. His head came off the bed and his stomach tightened to the point of pain. He lost all control and released inside her, flooding her until his own semen dripped out of her and back onto him. It was dirty and sexy all at once and he doubted Clover had any idea how much it meant to him that she let him come inside her body, how much it meant that she didn't simply let him, that she wanted him to, that she liked it no matter how messy it was. Life was messy and he wanted life with this woman, a long and messy and happy one.

With a sigh of contentment, Clover rolled off Erick and lay on the bed with her eyes closed and a smile on her face.

"Okay," she said. "I am now officially the happiest woman on earth."

"That's a relief," he said, then licked her nipple for no other reason than it was there, it was beautiful and he could. "I can call my weird kid again. She might ask for it in writing."

"I'll write it down. I'll write it down in triplicate and get it notarized. And you can go carve it in cedar— Here Lies Clover Greene, Happiest Woman on Earth."

"Carved in cedar? That's permanent, Clover."

"My happiness is permanent. Nothing can bend it, break it or ruin it."

"I can ruin it."

"No, you can't," she said, looking at him through narrowed, suspicious eyes.

"I can ruin it in one sentence."

"Try it. I dare you."

"Okay, here goes." Erick hated to see her happiness

dissipate but he had to do it. "Tomorrow is Thanksgiving and we have to go—"

"No, don't say it."

"I have to say it. We have to do it."

Clover groaned and this time it wasn't the happy sexy kind of groan. It was a groan of misery, pure misery.

"Say it," she said. "Wait." She grabbed a pillow and pulled it onto her face. "Now say it," she said from underneath the shield of her pillow.

"Tomorrow is Thanksgiving and…we have to…"

Clover groaned again.

"Go…"

The groan got louder.

"Grocery shopping."

Clover slapped both her hands onto the top of her pillow and pressed it down onto her face as if to smother herself. Erick easily lifted the pillow off her face.

"It's not that bad," he said. "It's early. We'll get dressed right now and go immediately. We can get in and out before the crowds show up. How's that?"

"But I don't want to get out of bed. Can't we stay here until, I don't know, Sunday?"

"No, we can't. We have to at least pretend to be grown-ups. I'm a parent. I've gotten very good at pretending to be a grown-up. You said your parents were leaving today. They could already be on the road to Oregon. They're going to expect turkey, yams, cranberry sauce and you and me putting on a damn good show of being happy to see them. Right?"

"You're right. You're definitely right," she said as she slowly dragged herself out of bed, the sheet wrapped around her like a bath towel again. "We might as well get this over with."

"That's the spirit."

"But you better have sex with me after grocery shopping," she said as she shuffled off to the bathroom, the sheet trailing behind her like a wedding dress train.

Erick reached down and grabbed the end of the sheet, pulling it off her with her next step.

Naked, she spun around and glared at him.

"That was rude."

"You're going to the shower and you can't shower in a sheet. I was only trying to help."

Sighing and shaking her head, Clover turned around again and once more headed to the bathroom on the second floor.

"You're lucky I'm in love with you," she said as she started climbing the steps, naked as the day she was born. "Or I'd be offended by this boorish behavior."

Erick rolled onto his back, smiling up at the ceiling. Knotty pine, beautifully finished, probably original. Wait.

What?

Erick sat straight up just as Clover disappeared through the bathroom door. He walked up the steps and tapped on the door.

"Clo?"

"What?" she yelled over the sound of the shower water coming on.

"Did you say you were in love with me?"

"Yes!"

"Okay, just checking."

"Is that a problem?" she asked. He heard the sliding shower door open and close.

He shrugged. "No. No problem. But you have to stop telling me stuff like this, you know, like this."

"Like what?"

"First, you told me you'd never had sex before while my penis was literally already inside your vagina."

"You brought it up."

"And then you tell me you love me on the way to the bathroom to get ready to go grocery shopping? You're kind of burying the lede here."

He heard more movement from inside the bathroom. The door opened and he stood back as Clover stood not only naked but soaking wet in front of him.

"I'm in love with you," she said. "I know we've only been together for four days but by my calculations we've spent over seventy-two hours in each other's company since Sunday evening. If your average date is four hours long—dinner and a movie, for example—then seventy-two hours is the equivalent of eighteen dates. And eighteen dates is more than enough time to decide if you're in love with the person you're dating. Most people know by the third date, I hear."

"I like that you did the math."

"I did. I'm a businesswoman. Businesswomen do the math. I realized it this morning while I was watching the sun come up and I felt so happy you were there. As beautiful as the lake is and the mountain and the trees and the sky, it was you being there that made me so happy. I thought you should know that so I told you first chance I got. Did I need to wait for a full moon or something?"

He peeked over her shoulder at her naked backside.

"Looks like a full moon to me."

"Can I get back in the shower now?" she asked. "I'm cold."

"I can tell. And yes, you can get back in the shower."

"Thank you." She turned around and started to close the door on him but he stopped it with his hand. She spun around again, hitting him with water from her hair. "Now what?"

"I—"

Clover slapped her wet hand over his mouth and, all of a sudden, he thought of another type of sex they should try.

"I don't know what you're going to say but I don't want you to tell me that you love me, too," she said. "I mean, I do, but if you said it now, I wouldn't believe you meant it. I'd be afraid you said it because I said it. I want you to say it when you're ready, not just because I said it. Got it?"

He nodded behind her hand.

"Good," she said. "Do you have something to say to me that isn't a declaration of love?"

He nodded again.

"Okay," she said, removing her hand. "Say it."

"I want to fuck you in the shower."

"You can," she said. "But not today. We're in a hurry."

She shut the door in his face, and he sighed the sigh of a man with an erection and nowhere to put it. But the sigh turned to a smile when he remembered this— Clover was in love with him. Well, damn.

While Clover was in the shower he pulled on his clothes and found his phone. It was only six thirty, which meant Ruthie would be asleep for, oh, five more hours at least. Now was a good time to text her since she wouldn't see the message yet.

Clover is officially the happiest woman on earth, he typed. You aren't allowed to give me the silent treatment anymore.

He hit Send with a smile, then set the phone down to start making coffee. He'd had his back turned to the phone for only a few seconds when it buzzed with a reply.

Good, Ruthie wrote back. Glad to hear it. I approve this message.

Why are you awake so early? he replied.

Unfortunately not for the same reason you are.

Get your mind out of the gutter. We're going grocery shopping before the crowds hit the stores.

Suuuuuuurrrrreeee…

Go back to sleep, he ordered. It freaks me out when you're awake during the day. Be a vampire like a normal teenager.

I had a busy night maiming and killing people on the dark sordid streets of Hollywood.

That's nice, dear. Hope you had fun. Glad you're talking to me again. Miss you, kid.

Ew.

You know you miss me.

Go kiss your girlfriend and leave me alone.

I will definitely do that. Have a good Thanksgiving. Tell everyone I said hello. Love you.

He set his phone down again, not expecting any further messages from his daughter, who had very likely stayed up all night playing violent zombie-themed video games with her brother and hadn't yet gone to bed. But he heard the buzz again and picked up his phone.

Are you and Clover really a couple now? Ruthie had written, and Erick sensed her anxiety in the question.

We are. Is that a problem? We can talk about it if it is.

No, it's cool, she wrote back. Then she sent him another message right after. I love Clover.

I know you do. I'm pretty crazy about her, too.

I was wrong when I said you aren't good enough for her. I'm sorry. You two will be great for each other. I'm actually kind of stupid happy about it.

Erick stared at his phone and blinked a few times. Did his child actually use the words *I was wrong* and *I'm sorry* to him? She did. It was right there in black and green.

That means a lot coming from you, he replied. I feel a great deal of fatherly affection toward you right now. I might even pay your cell phone bill without yelling at you for going over your text limit again.

But...just so you know, if you hurt Clover, I will honor the bonds of sisterhood over childhood and set your truck on fire.

I'm canceling your cell phone, he wrote back, and then took his own advice and switched the phone off. But not before Ruthie sent him one final message. Just the word *No* in all caps with approximately seven thousand *o*'s. Some days it was good to be the dad.

WITH ERICK'S HELP, Clover survived the grocery shopping trip. It was busy but not packed when they arrived and they were able to buy everything Erick said they needed before the real crowds turned up. Erick had picked up all his grilling stuff from his house and brought it over to hers, setting it up on the deck he'd repaired on Monday.

He looked right standing on her deck, setting up his Big Green Egg and waving at her when he caught her looking. He looked right on her deck, right in her house, right in her life. She hoped her family would see him the way she did. He was a good man, a good father and a good person with a big heart. It was so obvious how great he was, and yet Clover couldn't shake the feeling that tomorrow was going to be a disaster. Her family didn't say what they meant like Ruthie and Erick did. They spoke in a sort of code that disguised insults as compliments and questions as disapproval. Her mother had mastered the art of smiling and asking, "You're wearing that?" in such a way that those three words conveyed better than a billboard the message, "You aren't wearing that, ever, not if I have anything to do with it and it's your funeral if you do because you'll be dead to me." It was actually pretty impressive how much subtext her parents and her siblings could fit into so few words.

She couldn't think about that now. She thought about salad instead as she made a grape-and-walnut salad from a recipe she'd found on the internet. Erick had made a list of all the Thanksgiving basics and he'd promised to help her make them. Except for the brownies for dessert. Those she could make with her eyes closed. Her nieces and nephews would be thrilled to have Aunt Clover's brownies and ice cream for dessert while everyone else ate pumpkin pie. She'd never made a pumpkin pie before but Erick swore to her it was easy as, well, pie. He'd made them every year for Ruthie's school's fall festival since it was Ruthie's favorite dessert. Another thing to love about Erick—he was a great dad to Ruthie. Maybe other men wouldn't be comfortable raising a girl on their own, learning to bake pies for school events and going to PTA meetings, but Erick didn't seem to mind. He'd said he hated the term *Mr. Mom* because it implied that fathers who cooked and cleaned and helped with homework were exceptions instead of what they should be—the rule. She comforted herself with the knowledge that Erick had survived raising a complicated and difficult child with a penchant for arson all on his own and had come out on the other side with a healthy sense of humor and a daughter who'd put her pyromaniac ways behind her. If anyone could survive running the gauntlet of her family on Thanksgiving it was Erick.

The only question was…would she survive running the gauntlet of her family?

She was going to need a whole lot more lavender wipes.

Erick kicked her out of the kitchen around three in the afternoon with orders to rest. She didn't take orders well but she did stay out from underfoot by vacuuming, dusting and putting the extra leaves in the table to accommodate the whole family minus the kids who would eat either on the deck if the weather was nice or in the living room if it wasn't.

When everything was finished, they went out for Thai food for dinner and came home to her house, ready for bed by nine. Not for sleep, but definitely for bed. After Erick had worn her out with some vigorous sex, they settled into sleep. Very quickly, she'd gotten used to falling asleep with Erick's arm draped over her side and waking up with him next to her. She wanted to fall asleep like that, wake up like that, every day and every night. He'd told her today that Ruthie was "stupid happy" they were together, which made Clover "stupid happy." Now if they could only convince her family they, too, should be happy for them instead of digging and picking and looking for something to dislike about Erick.

"You're stressing out again," Erick said into her ear. "I can tell."

"How can you tell?" she asked.

"You're huffing a lavender wipe like it's an oxygen mask and your plane just lost cabin pressure."

"I hate that my family does this to me," she said. "I wish I could enjoy having them around instead of panicking about what they'll say to you."

"What's the worst that could happen? They hate me?"

"Yes. And that is the worst. Because I love you."

"I'm not sleeping with your parents or your sister or your brother. I mean, I might, but I'd like to get to know them first."

She slapped his hand.

"Fine. I won't sleep with any members of your family," he said. "My point is…if they hate me, who cares? As long as you like me, that's all that matters. You do like me, don't you?"

He slid on top of her.

"I kind of like you," she said. "A little."

"Are you sure you only like me a little?" He pushed her thighs open with his knees.

"I'm warming up to you."

"Maybe you even love me a tiny bit?" He settled on top of her with his cock only an inch or two inside her. She lifted her hips to take all of him into her.

"Maybe a little…"

Erick made love to her until she admitted once again that she did, in fact, love him. Worn out with sex, she fell fast asleep, distracted by her happiness. She woke up the next morning rested and refreshed from a good night's sleep. She dressed in jeans and her favorite navy blue turtleneck. Erick wore his khaki cords and her favorite long-sleeved navy blue sweater of his, the one that accentuated the broadness of his shoulders so well. They spent all morning in the kitchen mashing potatoes, stirring cranberry sauce and baking bread.

At one o'clock on the dot, Clover heard the sound of a car on her gravel driveway. Her stomach sank and her throat tightened. Erick bent and gave her one last kiss for luck.

"Here we go," she said.

"It's going to be fine," he said. "No scenes. No drama. And nobody is going to be mean to either of us."

The doorbell rang and Clover took a deep breath, put on her best fake smile and opened the door.

Her mother and father stood on the front porch. Her father had a suit on and her mother wore a tweed skirt with a white blouse and jacket. Chic as always.

"Hey, there," Clover said, holding the door open for them. "I'm so glad you're here."

"Oh, it's so good to see you, too, sweetheart," her mother said as she stepped through the door.

"This is Erick. Erick, this is my father, David, and my mother, Valerie."

"Everyone calls me Val, Erick," she said. "But I'll get to you in a minute. I have to hug this girl of mine first."

"Take your time," Erick said. "I'm not going anywhere."

Clover and her mother hugged and it was nice, comfortable. Maybe she'd been worried for nothing. Then her mother pulled back and looked Clover up and down. "Oh, so we're having a casual meal today, I see. Wish I'd known. I wouldn't have made the effort."

Clover forced her smile wider. She saw Erick's eyes flash in shock. All she could do was keep smiling as she hugged her father.

"I think she looks good, dear," her father said to her mother while they hugged. "Put on a few pounds since last time but you can't really tell."

Erick opened his mouth and she knew he was about to say something. She shot him a warning look.

"You weren't kidding," he said into her ear when her parents stepped into the office to take off their coats.

And she could only reply with three little words.

"Told you so."

12

ERICK SILENTLY REPEATED Clover's warning to him—"just grin and bear it, just grin and bear it…"

He grinned. He bore it. But he did not like it.

"So…" Clover said when her parents came out of the office. "This is Erick, my boyfriend. Erick, my parents—David and Val."

Erick shook hands with both of them.

"Very nice to meet you both. Clover's told me a lot about you."

"She hasn't told us much about you," Val said. "She's been a little hard to reach this week. Your doing?"

"Guilty," Erick said, entirely without shame. "We spent a couple days in a friend's lakeside cabin. Clover needed to unwind."

"Unwind?" David said. He was a handsome older man, well dressed and kindly looking, but Erick wasn't sure he trusted that smile. "What's got you wound up?"

"The usual work stuff," Clover said neutrally. "We closed up shop for winter so I wanted to take a couple days to rest. It was really nice. The lake is beautiful. Great cabin. Want wine? When are Hunter and Lisa and Kelly and the kids getting here?"

Clover spoke rapidly as if trying to drown her parents in a sea of words, changing the subject so fast they couldn't ask her any follow-up questions. Erick hated to see her so nervous, but he admired the strategy.

"I think they're coming now," Erick said, glancing out the window to see a black Audi driving down the gravel road toward the house. "Someone is."

"That's Hunter's car," she said.

"Hunter's the older brother," Erick said, looking at her parents, who seemed to be eyeing him very carefully. "Wife is Lisa. Three girls—Paige, Zoe and Skye. Did I get that right?"

"Very good," Val said. "Clover's been quizzing you?"

"She has. I wanted to make a good impression. I think she likes me." He smiled in the hopes of warming them up, charming them. Her mother only smiled tightly in reply.

"Any friend of our daughter's is a friend of ours," David said.

"Well, I'm her boyfriend, sir, not her friend. I hope any boyfriend of Clover's isn't a boyfriend of yours. No offense," Erick said. Clover laughed. No one else did.

Tough crowd.

Erick was relieved to hear car doors opening and closing. Hopefully the house would be full of kids soon and he could focus on them. He was good with kids. Kids loved him. Even better, kids weren't passive-aggressive and they usually laughed at his corny jokes.

Clover opened the door to greet Hunter and Lisa.

"Could you live anywhere more remote?" Hunter said as soon as he stepped across the threshold. "I hope that gravel didn't get in my undercarriage."

Something's in your undercarriage, Erick wisely did not say aloud.

"Gravel has never hurt my car," Clover said as she hugged Lisa, a pretty petite brunette. Another woman had accompanied them, a blonde just like Clover but taller and with shorter hair.

"Hey, sis," the woman said, stepping into Clover's arms for a hug. "Good to see you. You look great."

"Thanks. You, too." Clover turned to Erick and smiled. "This is Hunter, Lisa and Kelly, my sister. This is Erick, my boyfriend."

"Great to meet you all," Erick said, shaking hands with the women first and then with Hunter. Hunter was a big man, looked like a former football player, and when he shook Erick's hand he gripped it to the point of pain. Okay, then. Erick knew guys like this all too well. White collar suit with a need to prove his manhood since he worked behind a desk. Fine. Erick could handle that.

"Where are all the kids? Are they coming with Mike?" Clover asked. "Mike is Kelly's husband," she explained to Erick.

"Oh, did we forget to tell you?" Kelly asked. "My four are with Mike at his parents' house today."

"And our girls are with my sister," Lisa said. "Paige gets so carsick, you know."

Erick was grateful that Lisa at least had the decency to look guilty about not bringing her daughters to their aunt's house. Her sister? Not so much.

"I thought they were all coming," Clover said, looking wounded. He could see the hurt in her eyes, hear it in the crack in her voice. "I made them the brownies they love and we have stuff for s'mores."

"I can't believe we forgot to tell you," Kelly said. "That's my fault. Anyway, you don't have kids, Clo.

Your house isn't childproofed. I didn't think you'd have anything for them to do."

"Erick brought stuff to teach them how to make their own bird feeders," Clover said. "We had planned for them to come. I really wanted to see them."

"Aww...that's so sweet of you," Kelly said. "But you'll see them at Christmas."

"I was planning on spending Christmas with Erick and his daughter."

"Oh," Kelly said, looking the slightest bit sheepish— for once. "I hadn't thought of that. Well, you'll see them eventually. Lots of pics online in the photo album. Hey, Mom. How are you?"

"Happy to have all my kids under one roof," Val said, embracing Hunter and Kelly and smiling. "All my babies back together."

"You sent me fifteen text messages in the past two days and you couldn't have told me in one of those messages that you weren't bringing the kids?" Clover asked. Kelly pulled away from her mother's embrace.

"I just forgot, I swear," Kelly said. "I didn't think you'd care."

"Why on earth would I not care?"

"Well, you're not really a kid person," Kelly said.

"I love my nieces and nephews. You know that."

"Loving them and wanting them in your house full of breakable objects and poisonous plants are two very different things," she said.

"The only toxic plants are up in my bedroom," Clover said. "I don't care if they break stuff. Nothing here is really valuable."

"We'll bring them next time, I promise." Kelly said. "I just got so excited to meet your boyfriend I forgot to tell you. So what do you do, Erick?"

"I'm a contractor," he said. "Mainly cedar, decks and siding. That sort of thing."

"He owns his own business, too," Clover said, and the pride in her voice made him stand up a little straighter.

"That's great," Kelly said. "I always thought it would be fun to run my own business."

"Lots of work," Erick said. "But Clover knows that better than I do. I work alone. She actually has employees, and since one of them is my daughter, I know how hard she works at it."

"Too hard," David said. "Working her life away."

"I don't work that much, Daddy," Clover said.

"Gotta take time for yourself," he said. "Family is just as important as work."

"I took time for myself this week, and I enjoyed every minute of it," Clover said.

"Running off with a man and leaving your phone behind isn't exactly what I meant," David said.

"But it's exactly what I needed," Clover said, and Erick could see how shaky that plastered-on smile of hers was. There was only one thing for it.

"Who wants wine?" Erick asked. He did.

Erick went into the kitchen and poured out seven glasses of wine—two whites and five reds. Lisa slipped in and picked up two glasses for her and her husband.

"Let me get these," she said. "You only have two hands."

"Thanks for the help," Erick said.

Lisa glanced over her shoulder at the family talking in the living room.

"Word of advice," Lisa whispered, leaning in close to him. "Get out while you can."

"Too late," he said. "I'm in too deep."

"You have my sympathies," she said, then mouthed

the words, "Save yourself..." before putting on a fake too-wide smile and returning to the party. Apparently Lisa had about as much fun at these family gatherings as Clover did.

With that, she walked back into the breach, and Erick wondered if both glasses of wine were for her. For her sake, he hoped they were.

"Can I help in the kitchen with anything?" Val asked when Erick passed the wineglasses to everyone. He took a long deep drink of his red. Drinking might not be the best idea around this crowd but it would certainly help him put up with their sniping at each other.

"We've got it under control," Erick said. "Turkey's almost done. Everything else is warming in the oven."

"It all smells wonderful," Lisa said. "Thanks for having us. I wanted to host this year but then Hunter decided we needed to remodel the kitchen. Again."

Erick sensed they were drifting into choppy waters.

"Your fault you won't let me buy a bigger house," Hunter said. "So we remodel. Gotta look good for the bigwigs, right?"

"You finally learn how to cook?" Kelly asked Clover.

"Erick did most of it," Clover said behind her glass of chardonnay that she held in a white-knuckle grip.

"I admire a man who is good in the kitchen," Kelly said. "Mike is useless."

"Before the kid, I couldn't boil water," Erick said. "I had to learn fast after my divorce, and I got full custody of Ruthie. Kids have this weird obsession with eating real food multiple times a day."

"Mr. Mom," Hunter said, raising his wineglass in a mock toast. "Good for you."

"Not Mr. Mom. Just Dad," Erick said, putting on his most harmless smile. "Normal dad. That's all."

"Some men actually help around the house," Kelly said, leaning against her brother's arm. "Wild, right?"

"Sounds awful," Hunter said, shuddering in horror. "I work until six every day. I'm not going to come home and cook and clean, too."

"That's what I'm for," Lisa said with a too-bright smile. Her glass of red was already empty. "Plus dealing with contractors and decorators all the time…"

"Erick, do you think everything's ready?" Clover asked.

"Let's go check," he said. "You all will excuse us?"

Soon as they were alone in the kitchen, Clover put her forehead against the center of his chest.

"You're doing great," he said, stroking her hair. "Better than I would be."

"There's not enough wine in all the world," she whispered.

"We're going to make it. I don't know if Lisa is, but we will."

"Everything okay in here?" Val asked from the kitchen doorway. Clover stood up straight immediately.

"Great, Mom. What's up?"

"Came for a refill," Val said as she picked up the red wine bottle and topped off her drink. She'd hardly made a dent in her first glass. She wasn't there for a refill. She was spying on them.

"Well, dinner's almost ready," Clover said. "We'll start bringing stuff out soon."

"I'm sorry we couldn't meet your daughter, Erick," Val said, not taking Clover's hint. "I hope she's not missing you too much."

"She's seventeen. A week away from me is a vacation for the both of us. But you'll get to meet her eventually, I'm sure."

"Seventeen. That's a handful age," Val said. "Does she wear you out?"

"Not so much anymore," Erick said as he opened the oven door to check on the bread. All done. He put on oven mitts and pulled the pans out. "She got into a little trouble a while back, but working for Clover's been great for her. Helped her channel her energy into something constructive."

Clover picked up the sweet potato casserole and the three of them walked out to the table now covered in a fine white linen tablecloth and October-orange napkins.

"A little boy trouble?" Val asked as she laid down dish towels on the table where the hot dishes would go.

"I wish. That's what normal teenagers do. No, my daughter joined an ecoterrorist group online and set a factory farm barn on fire," Erick said. All conversation in the room stopped.

"She did what?" Val asked. Erick had to force himself not to smile. Ruthie was always good for getting a strong reaction, even when she wasn't there.

"Arson," Erick said. "She committed arson. But for a very good cause. She'd run away from home if she ever caught me buying non-cage-free eggs. A new factory farm was under construction and the group she belonged to decided to torch it before they finished building. It was a protest. She's a nature worshipper."

"So she's an environmentalist?" David asked.

"No, she's a literal nature worshipper," Erick said. "Neo-pagan, according to her. Although technically she says she worships Mother Nature but I've never figured out if that's an actual person in her theology. She can worship Gozer for all I care as long as she keeps her room clean and doesn't get arrested. Again."

"Well." Val blinked a few times. "What an interesting girl you have. You'll probably be relieved when she starts college. Do neo-pagans go to college?"

"Mine plans to," Erick said.

"And this girl works for you?" Val said to Clover.

"She's my assistant at the nursery. She's my best hire ever."

"I don't know what we would have done without Clover," Erick said as he placed forks, spoons and knives on the napkins Clover had laid out. "Ruthie got probation for the barn burning and had to pay ten thousand dollars in restitution for the fire damage. She emptied out her car fund and then had to get a job to pay the rest. No one would hire her because of her criminal record, but if she didn't find a job, she'd probably have had to do some jail time. The only thing Ruthie seemed to care about was the planet and nature so I thought maybe someone at a nursery would hire her. Clover was the only one willing to give her a chance. Still don't know why, but I appreciate it. For many reasons." He winked at Clover.

"She's so smart and driven," Clover said. "You just have to channel that energy into something positive."

"Your daughter is a miracle worker," Erick said to Val, hoping to counter some of the digs her family had taken at Clover with a few compliments. "Ruthie came back from the interview and said Clover was the coolest woman she'd ever met. I asked her why and she said, 'Clover says there's two ways of making the world a better place—you can destroy the bad or you can create the good. I think I want to focus on creating the good.' She's been a great kid ever since. All thanks to Clover."

"And you," Clover said, wearing a bright blush and the first genuine smile he'd seen on her face all day. "She's very lucky to have you in her life. So am I."

"She is," Erick said. "I tell her that all the time. Eventually she'll believe me."

"She believes it now." Clover gave him a quick kiss on the cheek as she walked past him to pick up her wineglass. Maybe they could make it through this day, after all.

"That's very sweet," Val said. "David, we might get to have a neo-pagan ecoterrorist for a stepgranddaughter."

"Hey," David said, lifting his glass in a toast. "Better than nothing, which is what we've got now."

"I don't know about that," Val said with a brittle smile.

Erick flinched as the wineglass in Clover's hand hit the floor and shattered into a million pieces.

"Shit," Clover said.

"Stay right there," Erick said. "I'll get the broom and the towel."

"You go check on the turkey, Erick," Val said. "I'll help Clover clean it up. Our little dropout is a bit dropsy today. Too much wine?"

"That was my first glass," she said. Clover was ghost white in the face. Had dropping the glass scared her that much? Erick looked at her but she wouldn't meet his eyes.

"I'll just, um, check on the turkey, then," he said. "Should be done."

He was alone on the deck for all of two minutes before Clover came outside.

"I'm so, so sorry," she said, looking like she was about to burst into tears. "I can't believe my mother said that about Ruthie. I can't—"

"Clover, it's fine," he said. "I'm fine. Ruthie didn't hear it. She's fine."

"I'm not fine," Clover said.

"I know, sweetheart. Look, I'm going to bring in the turkey. Everyone will eat and that'll keep them busy. We're going to make it. Just hang in there."

"Mom said something in the kitchen."

"What did she say?" Erick asked, keeping his voice calm. Clover was on the verge of losing it, he could tell. He didn't blame her. He was about ready to throw her over his shoulder, carry her out to his truck, drive off into the sunset, and never let her family within a hundred miles of her ever again.

"I told her she shouldn't say stuff about Ruthie like that and that you and I just started going out so even joking about Ruthie being her granddaughter made me uncomfortable. And she said, 'I just want the best for you, dear. Stepchildren are second-best and we want you to have the *very* best.'"

"Ouch," Erick said, wincing. "Wish Ruthie were here. She'd put your whole family in their place."

"Ruthie is not second-best," Clover said. "She's the best. Your daughter is the absolute very best."

"I know that and you know that, and God knows, Ruthie knows that. Who cares if your parents don't know that?"

"I care," she said. "I care, Erick."

He tried to say something else to comfort her, but it was too late. She had already gone back into the house.

Erick brought in the turkey on the platter and got out the carving knife and fork.

"You want me to do that?" Hunter asked.

"My turkey," Erick said. "My knife."

"You the man," Hunter said, raising his hands in surrender. Clover had put all the dishes on the table and everyone was taking their seats. Hunter sat at the opposite end of the table, the head.

"You're sitting in Clover's spot," Erick said.

"Am I?" Hunter said. "I always sit at the end of our table at home."

"It's okay," Clover said. "I'll move." She picked up her new wineglass and moved it from the head to the seat nearest Erick, who was considering telling Hunter that it was exactly where Clover had been sitting when he'd fucked her there on Monday morning. He thought better of it but at least the memory kept him from stabbing Hunter with the carving fork.

"So how's business going, sis?" Hunter asked. "You selling a lot of flowers this year?"

"Flowers and trees and garden equipment." She picked up her wineglass and took a sip of it. Erick saw her hands were shaking, but she was doing a good job faking a good mood. "In fact, I have some news."

"Good news?" Kelly asked as she sat opposite Clover.

"Great news," Clover said. "PNW Garden Supply offered to buy me out. I have until Monday to accept their offer. But it's a good offer."

"How much?" Hunter asked, leaning in and grinning.

"Five million," Clover said.

The room went silent immediately, a shocked silence much like the one that had greeted the news that Erick's daughter was a felon.

"Five million dollars?" Hunter repeated.

"Yes," Clover said.

"Jesus…" Hunter sat back. "I had no idea your business was worth anything."

"Gee, thanks," Clover said.

"You know what I mean," Hunter said. "That's a lot of money for some flowers."

"It's a nursery with two locations and over four acres

of prime real estate," Clover said. "I don't sell bouton-nieres to prom kids, okay?"

"Clover, that's fantastic news," Val said, clapping her hands. "Now you can stop working all the time and get your life together."

"And maybe give me some more grandbabies," David said, slapping Clover on the shoulder and kissing her on the cheek.

"What are you going to do with all that money?" Kelly asked. "Buy a bigger house? Travel?"

"Yes, baby, what are you going to do?" Val asked. "I'd say invest it. Hunter can help you."

"Sure, sis. You'll want to invest at least a big chunk of that money. Or are you planning on starting a new business?"

"Oh, God, I hope not," Val said, sinking into her chair. "Clover needs time off for herself. Not more work. She's thirty and it's time for her to settle down."

"You really should think about having kids," Hunter said. "Trust me, it's not as hard as everyone says it is."

"Seriously, though, Clo," Kelly said. "What on earth would you do with so much money?"

Clover glanced up at Erick and Erick met her eyes. She had a strange look on her face. She looked oddly... calm? No, not calm. She looked determined. She looked like she was about to say something that maybe she shouldn't say.

"Actually," Clover said. "I think I'll do what Ruthie suggested and blow it all on male escorts."

13

ERICK LAUGHED SO hard Clover thought he'd fall over. Not surprisingly, he was the only one in the room laughing.

"What?" Clover asked, glancing around the table at her family. "You don't like that idea?"

"You're joking," her mother said in that prim way she had of creating the reality she wanted to believe in.

"I'm not," Clover said. "I almost hired a male escort this week but then Erick volunteered his services."

"I'm much cheaper than Sven, and I come with a money-back guarantee," Erick said.

"Clover, this is not an appropriate topic for dinner," her father said.

"We aren't eating yet. Erick's still carving. By the way, Erick's my fake boyfriend, not my real one. I asked him to pretend to be my boyfriend this week to shut you all up about my personal life. Since it didn't work, might as well come clean."

"Wait a second," Hunter said. "What the hell is going on here?"

"Well…" Clover placed her hands flat on the table, pushed back her chair and stood up. "You see… I'm a very successful businesswoman who lives in a lovely little home in a beautiful community and I have a job I love and plenty of money. That is not good enough for anyone in this room except for me apparently. You all only care if I'm married and having babies for some reason. Or if I'm getting my PhD in something. Those seem to be my only two choices. But I'm not married, not having kids and not back in school. I knew you all would try to make me miserable about that so I needed a fake boyfriend. Erick volunteered. He probably wishes he were anywhere but here. And I don't blame him. I do, too."

"Clover Greene, this is absurd," her mother said. "Your family loves you and wants you to be—"

"Happy, right?" Clover asked. "You want me to be happy?"

"Yes, of course we want you to be happy," her father said. "That's all we've ever wanted."

"Then let me tell you how you can make me happy," Clover said. "You can shut the hell up about my life is what you can do and then I'll be the happiest woman on earth. Don't you all ever get tired of telling me what to do with my life, my body and my money? God knows I'm tired of hearing it."

"I will not be spoken to like this." Her mother stood up and faced her across the table.

"Don't like it?" Clover demanded. "Welcome to my world. You come into my house and insult my clothes, my boyfriend, my life choices and my boyfriend's daughter. Erick, you were right. They are all a bunch of assholes. Except you, Lisa. You're just a pushover."

"I know," Lisa said, and sighed.

"Takes one to know one," Clover said with true sympathy. "But I'm tired of being a pushover. Kelly, I love you, but you've been extremely bitchy to me lately and for no reason at all."

"What? I don't—"

"How many times have you told me I will never know true happiness until I have kids?" Clover demanded. "A hundred? A thousand? How would you feel if I said to you, 'Kelly, you will never know true happiness until you buy a house with your own money? You will never know true happiness until you've succeeded at making a business dream come true? You will never know true happiness until you can buy anything you want without having to ask your husband for permission?' You don't know that happiness because you've never paid your own way in your entire life. You got married right out of college to a rich guy. Mommy and Daddy footed the bills until you were twenty-one and your rich husband foots them now. Do you like hearing how you can't possibly be happy like I am? Do you like being told that I don't believe you're happy no matter how happy you tell me you are? You don't like it because it's an awful thing to say to someone, telling them they might never know true happiness."

Kelly opened her mouth and nothing came out. She covered it with her hand as if holding back words or tears or vomit.

"Damn," Erick said. He sounded almost impressed. "Direct hit."

"And you, Hunter," Clover said, "are a sexist jerk who treats his wife like a housekeeper. You tell me having kids isn't hard? You know why having kids isn't hard for you? Because you do none of the work. When's the last time you were alone with your three girls? When's the last time you took them to their doctors' appointments or cooked their dinner or even picked them up from school?"

"Never," Lisa said. Everyone at the table turned and looked at her. "What? It's true."

"You stay out of this, Lisa. Clover, that's not fair at all," Hunter said. "But what would you know about marriage and kids? You don't even have a real boyfriend."

"I feel real," Erick said. "Can you see me?" he asked Kelly and waved his hand in front of her face. She didn't even blink. "Okay, maybe I'm not real."

"My fake boyfriend I have been fucking all week long," Clover said. "Right where you're sitting, for example."

"Clover!" Her mother half gasped, half screamed. "How dare you—"

"How dare I? How dare I?" Clover asked. She was so angry she thought she would be sick. But the anger gave her power. She couldn't stop. Not when she'd finally found her courage. "You told me that I should break up with Erick because I deserve the best and a teenage stepdaughter is second-best. Did you not just say that ten minutes ago in the kitchen?"

"I only meant—"

"I know what you meant," Clover said. "Let me tell you how wrong you are. Ruthie is a goddess. On top of that, she's a friend. My friend. She's my friend and she's Erick's only daughter and for those reasons alone you should speak respectfully of her. What sort of adult woman insults a teenage girl behind her back? Especially a teenage girl I adore and respect and love. Ruthie isn't second-best. I would be the luckiest woman alive to be her stepmother. I'll tell you this, Mom. You don't deserve to be her grandmother. And you don't deserve to be her grandfather," she said to her dad. "How dare you tell me I've gained weight the second you walk into my house? Did I ask you for your opinion on my body? You look old, Dad. You look old and tired and wrinkly and gray and you're not as tall as you used to be, so put that in your pipe and smoke it."

Clover's father sat back in his chair and threw his napkin on the table.

"I think you sunk his battleship," Erick whispered to Clover. She ignored him.

"So, Daddy—how does that feel? Not good, I imagine, except I don't have to imagine because you all like to constantly remind me of my age. Thirty is a helluva lot younger than sixty-six, Daddy."

"Clover," Erick said. "Can I get you some water? Wine? Lavender wipe?"

"No, but you can get out of my house," she said to him. "You all can. Right now."

"Wait, I have to leave, too?" Erick asked, looking thunderstruck.

"My mother insulted your daughter to your face and you said nothing?"

"You told me to grin and bear—"

"I don't care what I said! They insulted Ruthie and you let them. I want all of you gone right now. Right this second. And don't come back until you've learned how to behave like human beings."

She turned her back to them and walked up the stairs and into her bedroom. She slammed the door behind her and locked it.

Then she sat down on the edge of her bed, the bed she and Erick had made love in just last night.

And she cried.

ALL OF THEM sat around the table staring blankly at each other. Erick looked from Mr. and Mrs. Greene to Kelly and Hunter and Lisa.

"Oh, I get it," Erick said. "Hunter Greene. Clover Greene. Kelly Greene. All shades of green. Clever."

Clover's parents and siblings all slowly turned their heads to stare at him.

"What?" Erick asked. "I just figured it out."

"What the hell just happened?" Kelly breathed.

"Your sister kicked our asses, that's what happened," Erick said. "A well-deserved ass-kicking from what I've seen. I think she's been holding that in for a long time."

"This is your doing, isn't it?" Val demanded of Erick. He could only laugh at that.

"God, I hope so," he said, standing up. Everyone at the table looked horrified, stunned, pale and angry. "Well, shall we?"

"Shall we what?" Hunter said, glaring at him from the opposite end of the table.

"Leave," Erick said. "Clover kicked us out. We have to leave."

"I am not leaving until I get an apology," Val said. She crossed her arms over her chest and looked as petulant as a small child.

"We're leaving," Erick said. "When you don't leave a house you've been ordered to leave, you are trespassing. We are trespassing."

"This is my daughter's house," David said. "My daughter."

"Yes." Erick nodded. "It's Clover's house. Not your house. I know all four cops in this town. I've worked on all their houses and given them all law enforcement discounts. Don't make me have to call them, because I will."

"Is that a threat?" Hunter asked.

"Pretty obvious it's a threat," Erick said. "Come on. Let's go. We can see if the mac-and-cheese place is open today. They have truffle fries."

"How can you be relaxed about this?" Val asked. She stood up and pushed her chair into the table so hard it would have chipped the finish if Clover hadn't put the tablecloth on.

"About what?" Erick asked. "Clover told us off. She didn't shoot at us. Has no one ever told you all off before? If not, might I recommend acquiring a teenage daughter? You can borrow mine. Do you think we should put the turkey away first? Nah. It'll be fine."

"I, for one, am happy to hear you aren't her real boyfriend," Val said. "I cannot believe my own daughter lied to me about dating you."

"She lied about dating me. I mean, she lied about not dating me. She is dating me. Or was," Erick corrected. "She might have just dumped me. Hoping she'll change her mind about that. But yes, until five minutes ago I was her real boyfriend. On Sunday she asked me to pretend to be her boyfriend but things got serious fast. I'm crazy about her. Even more crazy about her now." He stopped and laughed. "Man, this has been a wild week. Can't wait to tell Ruthie about it."

"A horrible week," Kelly said, finally speaking again.

"Buck up, little soldier," Erick said as draped kitchen towels over the food to keep any flies away. "You all got off easy from what I saw."

"Easy?" Kelly asked, staring at him wide-eyed. "You call that easy?"

"Every last one of you has been horrible to Clover since walking in the front door. Snide, judgmental, passive-aggressive and mean. I don't know why or where this is coming from, but I've known Clover for about a year and I know this—she doesn't deserve that kind of treatment. Nobody does. What does it say that your own sister asked a man to pretend to be her boyfriend just so she wouldn't have to put up with nosy questions about her personal life today? I think it says she doesn't like or trust her own family. She obviously loves you all, otherwise she wouldn't take your insults so personally. But she doesn't like you. I don't like you all, either."

"The feeling is entirely mutual," Val said.

"Fine." Erick shrugged again. "I think I'll survive. Coats are in the office. Let's get out of here."

"No way," Hunter said. "No way in hell am I leaving this house until my sister apologizes."

"You are leaving this house," Erick said as he pulled on his jacket. "And you're leaving it right now. First of all, Clover told you to leave. Second, she has nothing to apologize for. You all started this fight. Don't get pissed because she finished what you all started. Third, we really did fuck right where you're sitting."

"This is disgraceful," Val said.

"I didn't start any fight." Hunter did stand up but he didn't make any move to put on his coat and leave. Erick shook his head and willed himself not to put Hunter out of his misery. Men. "And I am not leaving."

"You said to your sister's face, 'I had no idea your business was worth anything.' Those are fighting words to me," Erick said. "You want me to walk into your office and say, 'So you actually have a real job, huh? Didn't think you'd amount to anything, Hunter.' You'd punch me right in the face if I said that to you, and you'd have every right to."

"I didn't...I didn't mean it like that."

"You said to your sister that you thought her business was worthless, and you were shocked when you found out it was valuable. Yes, you meant it. Yes, she was hurt by that. And yes, those were fighting words. If you make me throw you out of this house, I will do it."

"I'd like to see you try, buddy," Hunter said, pulling himself up to his full height.

"You might have been intimidating in high school," Erick said. "You look like you were one of those guys who threw freshmen into lockers. But this isn't high school. One of us has been working a desk job too long and the other one of us builds houses and decks for a living so... I know who I'd put my money on."

"Man, you are asking for it, aren't you?" Hunter demanded, his face getting redder.

"I am asking you to do what your sister said, and leave. I am not asking you to take a swing at me, but if you want to, go ahead. You'll miss and I'll have to hurt you. I don't want to but I will. I'm a contractor. I can put you through that wall, patch the hole and put cedar shingle siding on after. This house would look great with cedar siding so...go ahead, give me a job to do."

"Hunter, don't you dare start a fight," Lisa said, coming to stand between Hunter and Erick. "This is ridiculous. Erick is right. You all are rude to Clover. I've seen it with my own eyes more times than I can remember. You're bitter and jealous and I don't know why."

"We are not jealous," Kelly said. "Why would I be jealous of her?"

"No idea," Lisa said. "But you called me and talked me into leaving the girls with my sister for the day because you were mad Clover doesn't comment on all the pics you post of your children online. You said to me two days ago, 'If she doesn't care about our kids, why should we bring them to her house?' I can't believe I let you talk me into your petty little payback just because Clover's too busy to spend all day on Facebook validating your life choices."

"Oh, shit," Erick said. "Where is Jerry Springer when we need him? If someone's about to throw a chair, I want to record it. Where's my phone?"

"This is all so easy for you to say," Val said. "You're not the one who spent fifty thousand dollars sending that girl to college only to watch her quit school in the last year to sell tulips for a living."

"Now we're getting somewhere," Erick said. "You know college is a means to an end, right? The end being getting a good job. She got a good job without graduating and is now worth a lot of money. I get it." Erick pointed at Val and shook his finger. "You're mad because you thought she'd fail and go back to school, but she didn't, which proves she didn't need your help. Do you want your children to be dependent on you their entire lives? Is that why you're mad?"

"Fifty thousand dollars and she flushed that education right down the toilet," David said.

"Oh, yeah, poor Clover," Erick said. "She'll be worth five million dollars by Monday night, but yeah, I can see she really wasted her education."

"I raised three children and went to school at night for eight years to get my degree," Val said. "We handed her a college education on a platter and she threw it in our faces."

"Well...no," Erick said. "She didn't do that. I get that you and your husband are both academics. Clover told me. I get that you worked your ass off for your education. I get that you think that's the most important thing ever. But the money you gave your daughter for college was a gift. Gifts aren't supposed to come with strings attached. It wasn't a loan, it was a gift. She used that gift for a few years, decided she didn't need the gift anymore and then she got a job in a field she loves. If you gave her a car instead of a college education and she drove that car three years, decided she didn't want or need the car anymore and sold the car, would you be this bitter and angry? Would you?"

Val and David didn't answer. They looked at each other, both of them seemingly daring each other to say something, but they had nothing.

"Thought so," Erick said. "A gift is a gift. You all seem to think you gave her a fifty-thousand-dollar car and she got drunk and crashed it into your house, flipped you both off and ran away laughing into the night. She didn't waste the education you gave her. She just found a different way to use it."

"You don't understand anything," Val said. "Nothing at all about our daughter."

"I understand that when she told me about the buy-out offer on her business and I said, 'I'm proud of you,' she burst into tears because that's all she ever wanted to hear from her family. You busted your ass to get a PhD. She busted her ass to build a business from the ground up. Clover makes good money, she's a good person, she's a smart businesswoman, and instead of saying, 'Proud of you, Clo,' I hear you all mocking her for not being married, not having kids and not having a college degree. Are you all so insecure about your lives that you're threatened that Clover's happy without doing what you all did? Is that it? Kind of sounds like it. Could you maybe look at what Clover has instead of what she doesn't have? I don't have a college degree, either. I framed houses after high school, then got my girlfriend pregnant when I was twenty. I started my own company so my family could have a roof over their heads. Not a promising start, either, but now I have a job I like and a kid I adore and a girlfriend I'm madly in love with. You don't hear my parents telling me to get married and have more kids. They're just happy I'm happy. And with Clover. I'm happy."

"Erick?"

Erick turned around and saw Clover standing on the staircase.

"Oh, hey," he said. "Sorry. I'm trying to get everyone to leave. I swear."

"You're madly in love with me?" she asked in a small voice.

"Yes, ma'am." Erick grinned. God, it was good to see her.

She walked down the steps and he met her at the bottom. She threw her arms around him and he held her close and tight.

"I heard everything you said," she whispered in his ear. "All of it."

"Good."

"I heard everything they said, too."

"Don't apologize. Not yet," he said. "You can later if you need to but not yet. Let them stew."

"Excuse me," Hunter said. "We're still here."

Erick looked over his shoulder at Hunter.

"I see that. Why are you all still here?" Erick asked.

"I know how to get rid of them," Clover said.

"Brew coffee?"

"Not coffee."

Clover kissed him hard on the mouth. So hard and it

felt so good. He kissed her back just as hard. They made a show of kissing passionately, almost cartoonishly.

"Clover Elizabeth Greene!" Val said in a horrified huff.

Erick sighed and let Clover go.

"Ladies and gentlemen of Clover's family," Erick said, "we're about to have makeup sex. Probably on that couch. Maybe on the floor. I'd leave if I were you, but even if you don't, it's not going to stop us. Bye-bye."

He gave a little wave, then grabbed Clover around the waist and pulled her against him dramatically as any hero in any old Hollywood movie. He kissed her and kissed her and kissed her, not dramatically this time, not putting on a show to send her family scurrying. He kissed her as hard as he loved her and he loved her as hard as he kissed her, so it was no surprise they were both breathless by the time they looked up and saw Clover's family was long gone.

"Finally," he said. "Thought they'd never leave."

"Was I too hard on them?" she asked.

"You were incredible. Give them a few days to lick their wounds, then you all can talk it out calmly. But damn, you weren't kidding. They are awful."

"I wish I was kidding. I guess it didn't bother me that much when it was me, you know. But hearing them go after you, and after Ruthie especially... I couldn't stay quiet anymore. I erupted."

"Mount Hood's got nothing on you. And just so you know, standing up to your family to defend my daughter is the sexiest thing any woman has ever done. If I wasn't in love with you before, I fell in love with you right then and there."

"I thought I was in love with you before. And I was. But now...thank you for saying what you said, for defending me even after I kicked you out of the house. Sorry about that. I went a little scorched earth there."

"That's right, you did kick me out. I better go before you call the cops on me." He started to pull away from her and she grabbed him by the shoulders.

"Don't you dare leave me. We're supposed to be having makeup sex, remember? I've never had makeup sex."

"I have a better idea," Erick said as he picked her up in his arms and carried her up the stairs.

"Better? How better?"

"Much better. Makeup sex is good but there's one kind of sex that's better."

"Which is?"

He sat her on the edge of the bed and knelt on the floor between her knees.

"There's a kind of sex I haven't even had and I've done everything. It's the sex you have with the person you want to be with through everything—good and bad. I got married because I got my girlfriend pregnant, not because I wanted to get married. My other relationships never went anywhere. I haven't dated since Ruthie's arrest. What I'm saying is… I can imagine spending the rest of my life with you and I've never felt that about a woman before. I hope you feel the same."

Clover put her hands on his face and kissed him.

"Yes," she said. "I want to have that kind of sex with you. I've never been able to imagine spending the rest of my life with someone, either, but if my family disowns me and it's just you and me and Ruthie for the rest of my life, then that's not only enough for me, that's all anyone could ever want."

Erick kissed her again and started to push her back onto the bed. She stopped him with her hands on his chest.

"Just one thing," she said.

"Anything."

"Let's not get married for a very long time. It would make my parents too happy if we did."

"You're wicked," Erick said. "I love wicked."

He pushed her onto her back and pulled her shirt up to take it off. They froze when Clover's cell phone started ringing and beeping from the bedside table.

Erick picked it up and glanced at it.

"It's your mom," he said. "And a text message from your sister." The phone vibrated in his hand again. "And Lisa. What do you want to do?"

"You," she said.

Erick turned the phone off and jumped onto the bed. "They can wait."

14

CLOVER FELT IMPOSSIBLY light even with Erick on top of her. She felt clothed in happiness even as he undressed her. She felt joy even as tears slid down her face. More than anything she felt relief as Erick entered her and she lifted her hips to take all of him. He'd seen her at her worst, seen her family at their worst, and he loved her in spite of it all. And maybe even loved her a little because of it.

Erick moved in her with an almost unbearable tenderness, and Clover wrapped her arms around his broad shoulders, clamped her legs around his lower back and tucked her head against his neck. She'd liked him the day she met him when he came with Ruthie begging for nothing more than a job interview for his teenage daughter. He'd been so humble that day, almost scared, scared for his girl, who was facing real trouble. "Please, Ms. Greene," he'd said. "She's a good kid and smart. She's a real nature lover, and she'll work hard for you if you give her the chance." Clover had asked him about Ruthie's arrest and what he felt about it. When he'd answered by saying, "I don't believe in using arson or violence to solve your problems, but when I was her age, I spent my Friday nights getting drunk with my friends in someone's barn, not burning down barns to protest animal abuse. She made a bad choice, but she has guts and a good heart. When I don't want to kill her, I have to admit I'm proud of her."

I'm proud of her, Erick had said, and maybe that was the day Clover started to fall in love with him. About a year ago. But she'd loved Ruthie, too, which is why she'd hidden those feelings she had for Erick so well. It took Ruthie to bring them together, Ruthie to put them together, Ruthie to make them deal with their crushes on each other and get on with it.

"What are you laughing at?" Erick said as he braced himself over her and looked down into her eyes.

"Nothing," she said. "Sorry."

"You're not supposed to laugh while I'm inside you. It's hard on the hard-on."

"I wasn't laughing at you or your hard-on, I swear."

"Then what?"

"I was just thinking about Ruthie."

He raised his eyebrow so high Clover laughed again.

"That is a weird thing to do while we're having sex."

"I was thinking… I'm going to give that girl a raise."

"Unless you sell the company."

"Oh, yeah." She sighed. "I'll figure that out tomorrow. Today I just want to think about you. And turkey."

"We did forget to eat, didn't we? Sex first and food after?"

"Okay," she said. "But hurry. I'm starving. Fuck me fast so we can go eat all the meat and pie in the house."

Erick dropped his head to his chest and playfully wiped a tear from his eye.

"What?" Clover asked.

"'Fuck me fast so we can go eat all the meat and pie in the house'? Clover, I've waited all my life to hear those words from a woman."

ERICK WOKE UP alone in the bed. He'd done as Clover had instructed and fucked her hard and fast, but as usual he'd succumbed to a nap afterward. He strained his ears, curious where she'd gone. Bathroom? Kitchen? She had better not be eating without him. He found his khakis and pulled them on.

When he found Clover he thought she was crying. She sat on the edge of the guest bed with her back to him. She had her big yellow bathrobe on and her head was bowed. But then he heard her speaking.

"Mom, it's okay, really. Please don't cry. I'm not angry anymore. I just want our relationship to change, for the better. It has to because it can't go on like this. The way you treat me is unacceptable."

Clover paused and Erick went into the bedroom, sat down at her side. Clover leaned her head against his shoulder and it felt so good to be leaned on by this woman he loved he could have stayed there forever.

"I feel like I've been trying for nine years to get you all to listen to me, and when talking didn't get the message across, I yelled. No, I don't hate you all, not at all. I love you all. I love you and Dad. But today has to be the last day you bring up that I dropped out of college. The very last day. And you are never to call me your 'little dropout' again. Never and I mean it. It also has to be the last day you tell me who I should date or what I should do with my money. I'm not going to put up with it anymore, okay? You all raised me and you did a good job. Trust that you did such a good job that I can make my own decisions about my life."

Clover paused again and listened for a long time. He felt her swallowing hard.

"Thank you, Mom. I needed to hear that. I'm proud of you, too. Where do you think I learned how to work so hard? It was from you."

Clover wept softly against his shoulder and he kissed her on the forehead, rubbed her back, which was shaking under the strain of having this long-overdue conversation with her parents.

"Yeah," Clover said. "Erick's something. Better get used to him, though. He's going to be around for a long time."

Erick grinned but he couldn't help but wonder what her mother was saying to that bit of news.

"I like that he stood up for me, too. I promise, Ruthie is the best. She wants to be a college professor someday. You two will have a lot to talk about."

He left her alone in the guest room but only for a minute. When he came back she was finishing up her phone call.

"I love you, too, Mom. Happy Thanksgiving."

Clover ended the call and dropped the phone on the bed. After a long shuddering breath, she looked up at Erick standing in front of her.

"Told you they'd come around," he said.

"They are. Slowly."

"You ready to eat?"

"I am. First, I just need a—"

"Lavender wipe?" He held one out to her and she smiled and took it from his hand.

"You are the best fake boyfriend ever."

"Better than Sven?"

She stood up and tossed the lavender wipe over her shoulder. Who needed aromatherapy when she had Erick's sex therapy?

"Sven who?"

15

IF BEING ERICK's girlfriend didn't feel official before, it certainly did now. Clover stood at the Portland International Airport security exit as she waited for Ruthie to appear. Erick was in the car in short-term parking so Clover and Ruthie would have a few minutes alone to talk.

Funny. Clover had one day left to decide if she wanted to sell to PNW Garden Supply and yet the only thing that made her nervous was facing Ruthie. Erick had said Ruthie was happy for them, "stupid happy" even, but that was a few days ago and while Ruthie was in LA. When Ruthie saw her dad and Clover together it might be more uncomfortable than Ruthie had realized at the time. Clover couldn't stomach the thought of being happy at the expense of Ruthie's feelings. She could only hope that Ruthie could handle her father dating her boss, because the only thing that would suck more than losing Erick's love would be losing Ruthie's. Clover crossed her fingers, and if she could have, she would have crossed her toes, too. She had on rain boots, however, and they didn't have enough wiggle room in the toes.

Clover put on a bright smile as Ruthie turned the corner. In one week she'd changed her hair from purple to royal blue. Hello Kitty and My Little Pony stickers covered her rolling suitcase, and she wore black-and-white-striped leggings that made her look a little like Beetlejuice. She was impossible to miss.

Ruthie spied Clover and a bright smile crossed her face. Instead of walking, she jogged down the rest of the exit way to Clover and caught her in a huge hug.

"Mommy!" Ruthie said, squeezing the breath out of Clover.

"Oh, my God, the California sun fried your brain," Clover croaked.

"I'm just so happy to have a new stepmother." Ruthie sighed, leaning her head on Clover's shoulder and fake-weeping in her hopefully-not-fake happiness. "And just in time for Yule. We can celebrate the Goddess Rite together—stepmother-goddess and stepdaughter-goddess."

"I'm not your stepmother yet. Or a goddess."

"Ha! You said *yet*."

"Do we sacrifice people during the Yule Goddess Rite because I already have someone picked out if we do."

"No sacrificing. You just have to put on a crown of holly and a robe, say some ancient stuff and light the yule log. Then we bake cookies. But not for Yule. Those are for Christmas. Pops is a square. He won't let me cast a Yule circle unless we can bake Christmas cookies after."

"That's a good compromise. Your father is a wise man."

Ruthie finally released Clover, who took a full breath since she could again.

"He's dating you so I have to raise my low expectations of him," Ruthie said. Clover took the large backpack from Ruthie and they headed toward baggage claim.

"I'm glad you're not freaking out over us dating," Clover said. "I can't believe how fast everything happened."

"Fast?" Ruthie rolled her eyes and shook her head. "You two have been making gaga eyes at each other for a year. I thought I was going to have to cast love spells on you both to get you to admit it to each other."

"No love spells required. Just you forgetting your phone. Nice trick."

"I was pretty proud of that one myself. Took an insane amount of self-sacrifice on my part. I was phoneless for thirty-six hours. Now I know what life in the '80s was like. No wonder people were this close to nuclear Armageddon."

"Well, we appreciate your sacrifice on behalf of the cause. But I don't want you to worry. Your dad and I had a serious talk yesterday and there will be no moving in together or anything of the sort until you're in college. We don't want to mess with your routine."

"That's evil," Ruthie said. "Pops is evil."

"How is that evil?" Clover asked as they stood by the baggage claim belt waiting for Ruthie's other suitcase to appear.

"Pops is rigging the game so I have to go to college or you two won't move in together. And since I want you two together, I have to go to college."

"Trust me, gentle manipulation is preferable to parental passive-aggression. I speak from many years of experience."

"Yeah, how did Thanksgiving go with your family?"

"Your dad didn't tell you?"

"All he said was it was more a Spanks-giving than a Thanksgiving, but he'd let you give me the details."

"I told my entire family off and kicked them out of the house."

"Dammit." Ruthie sighed. "I always miss the good fights."

"Don't swear, dear," Clover said. "It's not ladylike."

"Yes, Mommy Dearest."

Erick met them in the parking lot and Clover was relieved to see father and daughter immediately fall back into their affectionate bickering and snarking at each other. No awkwardness. No weirdness. Erick complimented her Smurf hair. Ruthie ordered him to trim his beard before someone mistook him for a hipster, the lowest form of life in Ruthie's opinion.

"I'm thinking of shaving the beard and doing the waxed mustache thing," Erick said, putting Ruthie's suitcases into Clover's car trunk. "Thoughts?"

"No," Ruthie said. "Clover?"

"I've always had a little crush on Poirot. But you'll have to shave your head, too."

"Done," Erick said.

"I rescind my permission for you two to date," Ruthie said from the backseat.

"It was fun while it lasted," Clover said. "Thanks for playing."

"All my best to you in your future endeavors." Erick shook Clover's hand.

"Oh, shut up," Ruthie said. "You two are so cute it's gross. Please take me home. I need a shower and all the leftover turkey."

"We have nearly twelve pounds left over," Clover

said as Erick pulled out of the parking lot. "I kicked my family out before we could eat."

"And you didn't let them come back?" Ruthie asked.

"Nope. I wanted to but your dad said I should make them sit on it awhile. He was right. By the end of Friday night they'd all called me to apologize. Even my brother, who never apologizes. And poor Kelly—turns out she and her husband are having trouble. Mike wants more kids and she doesn't. They've almost separated over it."

"So that's why she's been trying to shove her happy-wife, happy-life crap down your throat for the past year?"

"I think she was trying to convince herself how perfect her life was. She and Mike are going to counseling. She said me yelling at her was a wake-up call for her. Of course she would take my pain and suffering and make it about her, but hey, baby steps, right?"

"I'm proud of you, Clo. Kicking your family out is baller. Bring it here." Ruthie fist-bumped her from the backseat.

"You're just happy we have so much leftover food," Erick said.

"This is Woman Bonding time. Men do not have permission to speak," Ruthie said, snapping her fingers shut like a trap.

"Ahh…now I remember why I was so happy when I put you on that plane," he said with a sigh.

Ruthie shushed him and turned her attention to Clover again, mouthing the word *men* and rolling her eyes.

"But speaking of people being selfish…are you selling the nursery?" Ruthie asked. "I need to know if I have to go to work tomorrow."

"You have to go to work tomorrow," Erick said.

"Shush, drone. Your part in the cycle of life is done. Clover?"

"You have to go to work tomorrow," Clover said. "Even if I do sell the nursery, ownership won't transfer for several months."

"If? So you haven't decided yet?" Ruthie asked.

"Nope."

"Good. I have to tell you something. This might sway you."

Clover heard Ruthie digging through her backpack.

"Here." Ruthie thrust a pile of papers into the front seat.

"What's this?" Clover asked as she flipped through the pages.

"Evan and his friends were driving me crazy yesterday. I had to get out of the house or I would have murdered them all, literally. So I went to the library and researched PNW Garden Supply. Turns out they were cited repeatedly for discharging pollutants at their wholesale nursery in Vancouver a few years ago."

"What? Why am I just hearing about this?" Clover asked as she riffled through the pages.

"They sold that nursery two years and two months ago, and they only had to disclose the past two years of business records. I'm guessing they want to buy Clover's Greenery and use that name to cover up their past environmental violations. It's not your fault you didn't find it. It wasn't in any of the paperwork they sent us."

"How did you find this stuff?"

"I have connections," she said with a smug smile.

"Are these the same connections that talked you into torching a factory farm?" Erick demanded. "The same connections you're forbidden from having any contact with?"

"Yeah, well, that's why I went to the public library to talk to them. Public computers. No record of our little chitchat," Ruthie said.

"My daughter is Edward Snowden. This is terrifying," Erick said.

"If i'm anyone I'm Mata Hari," Ruthie corrected. "And I was only doing it to help Clover. If you do sell to them, I'd make sure you have a long talk with the company about their environmental record and get some stuff in writing."

Clover took a deep breath.

"Wow. Guess I'm keeping the business," she said.

"You sure?" Erick asked.

"I'm sure. I wouldn't want my name attached to a company that can't clean up after itself. The Mount Hood location is on the edge of the Sandy River. The Portland location is a stone's throw from the Willamette. I'd never forgive myself if ammonia from the fertilizer or something worse got into the watershed."

"You feel okay about this?" Erick asked.

"Better actually," Clover said. "I hated not knowing what to do. And we're making good money. Not 'five million dollars' good but good enough to stay in business and keep the bills paid."

"Do you feel 'hire an assistant manager' good?" Ruthie asked. "Now that you and Pops are together, you should probably cut back on the eighty-hour workweeks. Even if you weren't together, you should probably cut back on the eighty-hour workweeks. Just saying."

"Don't nag Clover," Erick said. "It's her business. Her decisions."

"Oh, my Goddess, you have learned something from me," Ruthie said. "I'm so proud of you, Pops. You can teach an old dog new tricks."

"Thank you?" Erick said. "I think?"

"What do you think. Erick?" Clover asked. "What's your opinion on me hiring an assistant manager? I'm asking so I want your thoughts as a fellow business owner."

"I think hiring an assistant manager is a good idea," Erick said. "And we're only saying this because we care, not because we're criticizing. Your work ethic is impressive, but I would like to see my girlfriend more than one hour a week. And a business needs more than one person who knows how everything works. You could get hit by a bus, you know."

"Or pregnant," Ruthie said. "Because of the lemon tree."

"I don't want to know what you two have been doing with the lemon tree," Erick said. "So don't tell me."

"I'm not getting pregnant, Ruthie. But I will hire an assistant manager," Clover said, relishing the idea of having a personal life again. No more living for work. Time to start working to live. She'd hire a new manager, but not for Erick's sake and not for her parents' sake and not for the sake of any future children she may or may not have. But for her sake and her sake alone. "I'll start looking for somebody on Monday."

"Tomorrow is Monday. Do I really have to be there on Monday?" Ruthie asked.

"As a thank-you for digging up this stuff for me, you can have the day off—paid," Clover said.

Ruthie cheered from the backseat.

"Thanks, Clo. You're the best," Ruthie said.

"Yes, she is," Erick said, taking Clover by the hand.

Clover felt warm from the inside out, relaxed, happy, at home. She felt like she always wanted to feel with her family—loved unconditionally. Even if her own family still had some work to do, at least she could get that kind of unconditional love here, with Erick and Ruthie.

Erick kissed the back of Clover's hand.

"So..." Ruthie asked. "When are you two getting married?"

Clover looked at Erick, who winked at her.

"Ruthie, you're fired."

* * * * *

Want more sexy holiday fun?
Read the third book in Tiffany Reisz's
MEN AT WORK *trilogy,*
ONE HOT DECEMBER,
available December 2016,
only from Harlequin Blaze!